WISHING ON WINTER

JUNIPER CREEK GOLDEN YEARS
BOOK THREE

BRENNA BAILEY

Happy reading!

♡ Brenna B.

BOOKMARTEN PRESS

Published by Bookmarten Press

Wishing on Winter

ISBN (eBook): 978-1-7781867-7-6
ISBN (paperback): 978-1-7781867-8-3
ISBN (large print paperback): 978-1-7781867-9-0

Cover design by Cover Ever After
Edited by Jessica Renwick

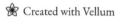 Created with Vellum

To everyone who feels like they aren't enough. I see you, and you are enough.

CONTENT WARNING

This book includes depictions of anxiety, depression, biphobia, and fatphobia. There are also brief mentions of cheating and drug usage. If these are difficult topics for you, please take the space you need from the story. You matter.

CHAPTER ONE

EVVIE

*E*vvie Adler was running late to her queer seniors' group —her own fault, since she couldn't tear herself away from the latest episode of her favorite romance writing podcast. The hosts were talking about using real life experiences to make characters authentic, and Evvie was musing over how to apply that to her current story.

She wasn't the only one running late. Two of her friends, Tom and Noah, walked into the center just as the podcast went into its final segment. The two men were holding hands as usual, and Evvie's heart squeezed painfully. It seemed like all her friends were paired up now—everyone except her.

When the podcast ended, she sighed, got out of her yellow Bug, and went into the community center.

As expected, the regulars were there already, sitting in a small circle of chairs near a table set up at the front. She'd seen Noah and Tom walk in, and Gem and Priya almost always got there early. They occasionally had a couple of extra people, but the five of them made up the group's core.

"There she is," Gem said, waving at Evvie as she walked to the table and poured herself a cup of tea. She grabbed a chocolate chip cookie and a napkin, then went to join the others. "I saved you a seat." Gem patted the chair beside her.

"Thanks." Evvie sat down. "What'd I miss?" She put her tea on the floor and handed her cookie to Noah, then she took off her jacket, smoothed her blue tunic, and crossed her legging-clad legs.

"We were just going through highs and lows," Priya said, tucking a strand of long gray hair behind her ear. Her salwar kameez was gray today, with splashes of pink, turquoise, and white. "Tom just finished telling us about their new hot tub."

Noah nodded, his hand on Tom's knee. "We were saying we should have everyone over for a hot tub party soon, before it gets too cold."

"*If* it gets cold," Tom added. "Even if it does, what's better than soaking in a hot tub while it snows?"

"I don't think my joints would like that anymore," Priya said, scrunching her nose.

"Mine either," Evvie agreed around a mouthful of cookie.

Gem, always the facilitator, turned to Priya. She had brought the group together, so it made sense for her to keep everything in order. "Priya, it's your turn. What's your high and low for the past week?"

Priya's eyes twinkled. "My high is the date I went on last night. We went out for dinner and drinks, then we had some . . . intimate time at her place."

"Good for you," Noah said. "So there will be another date?"

"Not with her, no," Priya replied, waving a hand. "That's my low. It was fun, but I don't see it happening again. There *will* be another date tomorrow night though, with someone else."

"Of course." Noah rolled his eyes.

Priya had been going on date after date lately, all because of Ember, a dating app designed specifically for seniors. "Anyway, enough about me." Priya looked at Gem and then Evvie. "What about you two?"

Evvie waved for Gem to go first since she was still finishing her cookie.

Gem shrugged out of her jean jacket and hung it on the back of her chair. "My high was going to Granville Island with Margie yesterday." Margie was Gem's girlfriend who lived in Juniper Creek—the same town Evvie lived in. It was only forty-five minutes or so from Abbotsford, where they met for queer seniors' night. Although Gem had been trying to get Margie to join their group, she hadn't yet. "My low was waking up this morning with a terrible crick in my neck."

"I keep telling you to try acupuncture," Priya said. "It works wonders." Priya's younger sister was a professional acupuncturist and had recently moved to Vancouver from Pakistan, so Priya was always trying to get them to use her services.

"Only if you're not terrified of needles," Gem shot back.

Priya shrugged.

"What about you, Evvie?" Gem asked, turning to her.

Evvie uncrossed her legs and recrossed them the opposite way. "My high and my low this week are so close, they're almost married. For my high, I found one of my old romance manuscripts from when I was determined to be a writer. I typed it up, and the story isn't terrible, honestly. It's lacking in feeling and there's no ending, but I think I can work with it.

"It's also a high because it gave me something to do, which brings me to my low: trying to settle into retired life. I've only been retired for a couple of weeks, but I feel like I'm floating around aimlessly. How do you all fill your time?"

Everyone else in the room had been retired before their group came together.

"We spend most of our time with each other, I think," Tom said with a fond glance at Noah. Tom had been diagnosed with Alzheimer's back in June, but he seemed to be having a good week, or at least a good day.

Gem shrugged. "I spend much of my time with Margie."

"And you know what I do," Priya said, waggling her eyebrows. "I date, I shop, I eat good food. I go out with friends. Never a dull moment."

Evvie chewed on the inside of her cheek. Her work at the animal clinic had filled her days—more than she had wanted it to —and when she wasn't working, she volunteered for events in town, or she spent time with her best friend, Dylan. But since the fundraiser to save the library had finished, Dylan had been spending most of her days with Frankie, her photographer girlfriend who had officially moved to town earlier that month. Evvie's other closest friends—Minnie and Eleanor—were another couple who spent most of their time together. Her friends still visited with her, of course, but their worlds had expanded to include their significant others. Evvie herself had no family to spend time with, and she didn't want to be the third wheel, or the fifth, all the time.

Under her breath, she said, "Everyone has someone except me." Not to mention, her seventy-first birthday was coming up in December—on Christmas Day, no less, which was her favorite holiday. Although her friends likely wouldn't leave her alone for it, it would be nice to have someone to cuddle with that day.

"Well, that's easily fixed." Priya widened her eyes at Evvie meaningfully. "It's not difficult to make an Ember profile."

Evvie's heartbeat picked up. She hadn't dated anyone since Simon had left her over forty years ago, and for good reason. Having your high school sweetheart cheat on you then tell you that you weren't enough for him did things to you. It was enough to make her move from Alberta to BC, putting an entire mountain range between them. And then to watch her best friend discover her queerness and go through her own divorce . . . Well, Evvie didn't have high hopes for herself when it came to love.

But maybe it was time to change that. At the very least, going on a date would give her material to work with for her novel.

"You know what," she said, looking around at her friends. "Let's do it. Let's make me an Ember profile."

Noah straightened up. "Really? I thought this day would never come." He looked wistfully at Tom.

"You were hoping for this?" Gem asked, an eyebrow raised in his direction.

"Not exactly," Noah said.

"He enjoys playing matchmaker for our friends," Tom added. "And he's always wanted to make a dating profile, but we haven't had the opportunity, being happily monogamous."

"Well, now you have an opportunity," Evvie said, shifting in her seat. The more she thought about this, the more excited she got. Priya seemed to have success with the app, and her other friends had found love in the past few months. Now it was her turn. Maybe she'd find someone to spend the holidays with so she wouldn't have to crash any of her friends' romantic plans. It was mid-November—she had plenty of time. "Let's do this."

Over the next hour, the five of them worked together to set up Evvie's dating profile. Gem grabbed a piece of paper so they could draft Evvie's bio, Tom and Noah looked through her phone to find flattering photos of her, and Priya gave everyone tips for what worked well in the app. Once they had chosen a photo and Evvie was happy with the bio, Priya showed her how to make her profile.

"You can make the font size bigger so you'll actually be able to read everything. Oh, you can pick your sexuality too, if you want." She showed Evvie a drop-down menu full of options. "It will help narrow down the people you can match with."

"Let me see," Evvie said, taking her phone back. She scrolled through the options. "Good gravy! I don't recognize most of these. There's a whole alphabet of choices in here." She scrolled back to the top and picked *bisexual*, which she felt comfortable with and understood. "Good enough."

"Perfect. Ready to go live?" Priya said, her finger hovering over the "done" button.

Evvie nodded. Priya pressed the button, and Evvie let out a squeal. "Now what?"

"Now you can wait for people to match with you, or you can browse through folks the app thinks you might fit well with."

"Can we browse?" Noah asked, practically bouncing in his seat. "I want to see what type of people use this thing." Tom patted Noah's shoulder as if to calm him down.

Gem scoffed. "This is *Evvie's* profile, remember, Noah?"

"I don't mind," Evvie said, holding her phone out for him to see. "Let's take a look."

They spent the next half hour browsing profiles, snorting at the ridiculousness of some people's photos and biographies while admiring others. With her friends' encouragement, Evvie clicked the thumbs-up button on a few profiles, sending a thrill through her. That tiny action didn't mean much, but she didn't know what she'd do if she got a match.

Evvie left the community center in good spirits, and she gave everyone a hug before she got into her Bug. "Thank you, all!" she called to her friends as they went to their cars. "I'll update you next week!"

She was practically vibrating as she settled into her seat and turned on a podcast. As she headed out for the drive back to Juniper Creek, her thoughts about potentially dating again were so loud that she shouldn't have bothered putting on a podcast at all—she didn't hear a single word.

CHAPTER TWO

MATTHIAS

The last thing Matthias Vogel expected to see as he went to get breakfast was a chicken wearing a diaper sitting at the kitchen table beside his sister. And yet there it was, and Loretta didn't seem fazed at all as she sat there, sketching and sipping a cup of tea.

"Um, good morning," Matthias said, heading straight for the coffee machine. There wasn't a time change between LA and the Fraser Valley, but he felt disoriented nonetheless. He'd been back here for less than twenty-four hours, and waking up in his child-hood bedroom had thrown him for a bit of a loop. He was used to opening his eyes to his bunk on the tour bus or in his spacious room in LA, not in the creaky house he'd left when he turned twenty-one. He swore the mattress was the same one he'd left back then, and it did nothing to help his aching back. It hadn't been comfortable when he was a teenager, and it wasn't comfort-able now when he was seventy-four. It was also low to the ground, which wasn't great for his bad knee.

"Good morning," Etta replied brightly, glancing at him. She ran a hand down the chicken's back, and the chicken leaned into her as if it enjoyed the attention. Well, at least Matthias knew the chicken was real and he wasn't hallucinating.

"Etta, why is there a chicken at the kitchen table?" he asked as the coffee began to percolate. He scratched an itchy spot on the back of his neck and hoped Etta wouldn't notice.

"The other girls were picking on Persephone, so I brought her in for a bit. She likes being in the house, anyway."

Matthias nodded slowly. "Right. That makes sense." It didn't make any sense, but who was he to judge? He knew nothing about chickens; his forte was playing the drums.

At least Etta seemed to be doing well this morning. Sketching was a good sign, and she'd made herself tea. Her long still-dark hair was pulled up in a bun, and she was wrapped in a fluffy housecoat, wearing matching slippers. She didn't seem as pale as she had the day before, either. Maybe his daughter Bea had been wrong about Etta's mental health . . . but she wouldn't have suggested Matthias come for an extended stay if she hadn't been truly worried.

"Have you eaten anything?" he asked.

"No," Etta replied. "I don't usually eat breakfast."

"Hmm." He grabbed a mug off the wooden rotating mug holder and filled it with steaming coffee, inhaling the nutty scent of it. "Since I'm home, why don't I make pancakes?"

Etta shrugged.

"Come on. It's not every day your older brother offers to make you breakfast. If you turn me down, I might never offer again."

She sighed. "Fine."

"Great." He got to work, trying to ignore the chicken—Persephone—as he mixed the batter. He stole a glance at her, and she seemed to stare straight into his soul, causing him to slop pancake batter on his flannel pajama pants. He scowled and glared at the chicken as he wiped himself off.

He adjusted his knee brace then opened the fridge to see if there was anything they could eat with the pancakes. He'd love bacon, but Etta was vegetarian, so there wouldn't be any in the house. There were plenty of eggs, of course, and a small container of just-past-good blueberries, but the fridge was almost empty other than that. He'd need to make a grocery run soon.

"Here we go," he said twenty minutes later, putting a plate of pancakes in the center of the table. He'd found syrup and peanut butter in the cupboard, and he slathered his pancakes with them as Etta daintily took one pancake and ate it plain. He frowned.

"Does Persephone want some?" he asked, eyeing the chicken again.

Etta flicked her gaze to his. "Don't be ridiculous. Chickens don't eat pancakes. I only feed them fresh food scraps and organic chicken feed."

It was all he could do not to roll his eyes. "Of course. My bad."

"Are you alright?" his sister asked, her green eyes full of concern.

"Yes," he said around a mouthful of pancake. "Why wouldn't I be?"

"You're scratching your neck and your arm."

He swallowed and avoided her look, taking a sip of coffee to wash down the peanut butter.

"Do you have stress hives?" she asked. She reached to grab his arm, his skin clearly red from where he'd been scratching, but he pulled back.

"What? No." Damn her for being so observant. The whole point of him being here was to keep her company and make sure she was okay; the last thing she needed was to worry about him.

"You do, don't you?" She sat back in her chair. "What's wrong? Is it moving home? I told Bea I was fine by myself. You didn't need to come, you know."

He sighed. He'd been trying to avoid this topic because not talking about it meant he could procrastinate longer. But if he didn't tell Etta the truth, she'd be even more worried. "It's nothing to do with you. After our farewell tour, an agent for some publishing house approached Colin about putting together a book about the band." Colin was the manager of Iridium

9

Twilight, the band Matthias had been drumming with since his early thirties.

"Oh?" Etta leaned forward with her elbows on the table, her pancake still mostly uneaten. Persephone looked at him with her head cocked to the side, and he got the eerie feeling she was genuinely listening to him. "Why is that stressing you out?"

"Because Colin thought it would be a good idea for us to write our own histories of the band then have a ghostwriter go through everything and compile the full story, taking bits and pieces from each of us."

"That sounds like fun. I'm still not getting the *stressed* part of this."

"Etta, I don't write. I barely graduated from high school, and I'm pretty sure I can read music better than words. Nick wrote all our lyrics. How the hell am I supposed to put together a coherent story of our band history?"

Etta nodded, a crinkle appearing between her brows. "Well, how much time do you have? Maybe we can work through it together."

It warmed his heart that Etta would help, but he didn't want to put that pressure on her. And once she found out the deadline . . . "I'm supposed to send it by January."

"That's in less than two months."

"I know."

"Have you started working on it yet?"

". . . I've been thinking about it."

Etta pursed her lips and gave him that look—the one that mirrored their mother's. Head tilted slightly, eyes widened, judgement practically shooting out of her pupils like laser beams. "Thinking isn't the same as doing, Matthias."

He groaned and hung his head. "I know."

He felt the weight of her hand on his arm and raised his head.

"You still have time," she said. "We'll figure it out, okay? Maybe you can use dictation or something."

"Okay." As he looked at his sister—still his *little* sister no matter how old they both were—his throat tightened. For once, he wanted to help her, not the other way around. But in less than a day, he'd somehow gotten *her* to help *him*. So much for being a good older brother.

"Finish your pancake," he said sternly, breaking the moment. She scoffed, and Persephone echoed her with a distinctly conde-scending *cluck*.

Too bad. If Etta was going to help him with his stupid band biography, he was at least going to make sure she ate properly.

CHAPTER THREE

EVVIE

*E*vvie stood at the printer in the library and shifted from foot to foot. Her manuscript was taking *forever* to print.

"You look like you have to pee." Dylan smirked at her from the front desk, which was accented with a green and red garland, signaling the upcoming holidays.

The library wasn't open yet, so Dylan and Evvie were the only people there—one of the perks of having a librarian as a best friend. Evvie appreciated the privacy; she didn't want anyone to know she was writing a book yet. Anyone other than Dylan, obviously.

"So are you going to hole yourself up in your house to revise that thing?" Dylan asked, coming over to stand beside Evvie. She was wearing her typical uniform of a black-and-purple plaid shirt, blue jeans, and her scuffed black sneakers.

"No," Evvie said, frowning. "If I try to work at home, I'll get distracted. I'm going to drive to one of the Abbotsford libraries and work there since the chances of seeing anyone I know are slim."

Dylan nudged her lightly. "I don't get it. What's the big deal about people knowing you're writing a novel? No one's going to care."

"Well, *I* care. You know what people in this town are like. They'll ask what it's about, and I'm not ready to talk about it. There's something missing from the story, I know it. I need to figure it out before I start telling people. Otherwise, I'll jinx the process."

Evvie didn't need to look at Dylan to know skepticism would be written all over her face. Eleanor and Frankie would understand, but not Dylan. Or Minnie either, come to think of it. But Evvie trusted Dylan the most, so here they were.

"You'll jinx the process?" Dylan asked, her tone heavy with disbelief.

"Yes." Evvie bent down and peered into the printer as if examining the printing would speed it up.

"O-kay." Dylan broke up the word into two distinct syllables. "Well, good luck on your revisions."

"Thank you." Evvie's phone pinged, and she pulled it out to see a notification from Ember. She tried to suppress her smile —*tried* being the key word. Opening the app, she saw a message from Antonio about their date on Wednesday.

A date! Evvie was going on a date!

Dylan moved closer to her, her chin brushing Evvie's shoulder as she leaned over to read the message. She shook her head. "I can't believe you're going on a date with someone you met on an app."

"Why? It's how all the young people meet these days."

"Yes, but we're not exactly *young* anymore, are we?"

Evvie scoffed. "I feel as young as I ever have."

"Lucky you. I wish my knees felt that way. Anyway, I need to open the door."

"It's nine o'clock already?" Evvie stared at the printer again, willing it to print faster. The manuscript looked almost finished, and she needed to get out of there before library patrons started showing up.

Finally, what seemed like an agonizingly long time later, the printer spat out the last page of her incomplete story. She scooped up the papers and gently tapped them against the table until they were neatly aligned. Then she tucked them into her winter jacket, keeping them pressed snugly against her chest, and headed for the front doors with a wave to Dylan. The snowflake decals on the glass sparkled as the doors slid open to let her out.

Once in her Bug, she set the stack on the passenger seat and smiled at it. She had written that manuscript. Every single page was filled with her writing, and it was surreal. Now to get it to a place where she could be happy showing it to someone.

She drove down Main Street on her way out of town and pulled into a parking spot in front of Dawood Bakery. In her excitement to print her manuscript, she'd forgotten to make herself coffee that morning. She'd get a headache if she didn't get some caffeine in her system before noon.

She had every intention of leaving her manuscript in the car, but it was her baby. She couldn't leave it in there alone, sitting on the seat in plain sight, waiting for someone to steal it. Once again, she scooped it up and held it against her chest beneath her coat, pressing one arm across her body to keep the story safe. Dylan would have toppled over with laughter if she could see what Evvie was doing, but Evvie didn't care.

There were three customers in line before her and one sitting at a table inside. Aaliyah was taking orders and bagging baked goods while Kamran, her husband, made drinks and rang people through. Evvie patiently waited her turn, admiring the small gold stockings and stars the owners had strung along the display case. She ordered a peppermint mocha and a muffin to go, wishing she had time to sit down and enjoy a bowl of Aaliyah's kheer. The Indian rice pudding dish had become a favorite of hers during fall and winter. Maybe she'd save that as her reward for when she finished her manuscript.

"Are you alright?" Aaliyah asked, glancing at Evvie's arm pressed across her ribs, holding her story in place.

"Oh yes, I'm perfectly fine."

When Evvie didn't elaborate, Aaliyah shrugged and got her muffin.

Keeping her manuscript safe—and hidden—was more difficult than Evvie had anticipated. She managed to hold her purse with the crossed arm and work her credit card out of her wallet, tapping it to pay. Putting the lid on her steaming hot coffee was another matter, though. Kamran saw her struggling and helped without a word.

"Thank you," Evvie said, beaming at him.

She turned around to leave, taking one step before—"Oof!"

She walked straight into someone coming toward the counter, her face colliding with their chest. Her coffee got smooshed between them and the lid popped off, sending hot peppermint mocha all down her coat.

But her manuscript . . . her manuscript!

As she stepped back in shock, the papers slid out from beneath her arm and the safety of her coat, the unclipped pages spreading across the floor like a paper tsunami. To her horror, the person she collided with had dropped their drink as well, and her pristine story pages were soaking up the liquid, slowly turning to mush before her eyes.

"Oh!" She covered her mouth.

"Shit, I am so sorry," the person said with a gravelly gasp.

Evvie blinked and looked up to see a tall man who appeared to be about her age, his sweater and jeans splashed with coffee. He leaned on a glossy red cane, the bottom of it now in a brown puddle. A trim silver beard framed his face, slightly darker around his mouth, and he had a matching mustache. His short hair was also silver around the temples but darker on top. Something about him looked familiar, but she couldn't quite place what it was.

"Are you alright?" he asked, his forehead wrinkled. Small creases fanned from his brown eyes. His voice was low and slightly gruff, and in any other circumstance, Evvie would have swooned. But not in this one.

It took Evvie a moment to absorb what he had asked. "I'm . . . I'm fine." Her manuscript, on the other hand, was not. She shoved the bag with her muffin into her coat pocket and crouched down, trying to gather the pages that were still dry. The wet ones were a lost cause.

"Let me help," the man said.

"No, it's alright," Evvie said, waving him off, but he was already there with a roll of paper towel that he must have grabbed from the counter. He tore sheets off and pressed them onto the soaking papers as if he could salvage them. He was clearly struggling to bend over, wincing as he moved.

Tears built at the back of Evvie's throat, but she ignored them. Her story wasn't gone; she could easily print it out again. She just needed to get these papers together before—

"Are you writing a novel?" the man asked, clearly reading a page he had picked up from the floor. "This is pretty good."

"That"—Evvie snatched the page from his hand—"is none of your business." The tears were gone now, replaced with her heart, which had leaped into her throat in a panic.

"You're right, I'm sorry. I haven't even introduced myself. I'm Matthias." He dropped the soaked papers and held out a hand as if they hadn't just collided, spilled coffee on each other, and soaked Evvie's manuscript into oblivion.

Automatically, Evvie reached to complete the handshake, but her fingers were sticky, and she'd left wet fingerprints on the pages she'd gathered. She shook his hand anyway. "Evvie," she said.

"Evvie, let me clean this up and get you another coffee. I wasn't looking where I was going. I'm so sorry."

Her instinct was to say no, she was fine, but her plans for the day had just gone out the window, so she collapsed into a chair instead and cleaned herself up with the paper towel.

Matthias used his cane and his foot to push paper towels around and soak up the remaining coffee, and Aaliyah came over to help gather the manuscript pages.

"Do you want . . . these are a bit . . ." She held the stack of dirty pages out toward Evvie, who shook her head.

"They're trash now." The words almost hurt to say, but there wasn't anything she could do about it. "I'll print new ones later."

Aaliyah gave her a sad smile and put the papers in the garbage.

Matthias looked like a puppy who'd been caught eating a roll of toilet paper. Evvie's anger at the situation evaporated as she looked at him, and she sat back in her chair, resigned.

"Here." Kamran came over with two fresh cups of coffee. "On the house," he said. Matthias protested and insisted on paying, but Kamran held up his hands. "Accidents happen. It's not a problem."

He went to grab a mop as Matthias sat in the chair across from Evvie and reached for one of the cups with a sigh. "Well, that's one way to start the day."

Evvie raised her eyebrows and grabbed the other cup. "You can say that again."

"I really am sorry," Matthias said. The coffee on his sweater had turned the burnt-orange fabric into a darker almost-red. Evvie had taken her jacket off and draped it over the back of the chair to dry.

"You didn't do it on purpose," Evvie said, waving him off. "I hope, anyway."

He laughed, and the sound made her feel better. Happy, almost. "If I did, I'd let you spill another coffee on me, no questions asked."

The corners of her lips ticked up slightly. "That would be a waste of coffee."

His grin echoed hers for a moment then fell. "Was it . . . what were the pages?"

Evvie licked her lips. What could she tell him? That she was a teacher, and the papers were stories her students had written? Or maybe that she was an editor and she still preferred to edit by hand? No, she couldn't lie. She *despised* lying. On the bright side, she had never seen this man before and likely would never see him again, so the truth probably wouldn't hurt.

"You were right. I am writing a novel." There, she said it.

"A romance novel, right?" Her confusion must have been evident on her face because he continued, "The page I picked up seemed like a happily-ever-after-type of scene."

"Oh. Yes, it's a romance novel."

He sipped his coffee and sat back in his chair, straightening his leg—it seemed rather stiff—and displaying one of his coffee-stained leather shoes. They looked expensive.

"There weren't any edits on those pages, I hope?"

She shook her head. "I had just printed them. I was going to start editing today, actually."

"Ah." He tapped the table a couple times with his palm. "Why don't I re-print them for you? There's a library down the road."

"No need. I appreciate the offer, though." And she did. The more she sat there with Matthias, the more she found herself relaxing. So what if she'd lost her manuscript pages? Things could have been worse.

She sipped her coffee then said, "I don't think I've seen you around town. Did you just move here?" He knew about the library, but Evvie didn't know him, and Juniper Creek wasn't that big.

He broke eye contact. "I grew up here, actually. I haven't been back in a while, but I'm visiting my sister."

"Your sister?"

"Loretta Vogel. She lives on a farm just outside town."

"Oh!" Evvie nodded. She'd met Loretta at a farmers' market years ago, and she'd seen her around town many times. "Yes, I know Loretta. I didn't know she had a brother."

Matthias shrugged and looked at his watch. "Speaking of Loretta, I'd better go. I was just in town to get a coffee and groceries. I'm sorry, again. Good luck with your novel."

"Thank you." As Matthias stood to go, Evvie had the urge to

join him, to shake his hand or give him a hug. But they didn't know each other that well, so she settled on a wave.

After he left, she called Dylan and asked her to re-print the manuscript. She ordered a bowl of kheer—she deserved a pick-me-up with how the morning had gone—her thoughts torn between her story and the man who had spilled coffee all over it.

CHAPTER FOUR

MATTHIAS

*G*uilt and a note of panic followed Matthias around for the rest of the morning—up and down the grocery aisles, on the drive back to the house, and as he brought the groceries in and put them away. He felt bad for running into Evvie, but why had he introduced himself? What if she had recognized him?

He was shelving the last box of cereal when he heard a *cluck* behind him. Etta stood in the doorway in her pajamas, holding a diaper-wearing chicken in her arms.

"Is Persephone getting picked on again?" he asked, trying to keep his tone serious.

"This is Circe, not Persephone," she said, scowling at him. "They look completely different. Persephone is red with brown mottling, and Circe is brown with red mottling."

He turned to the cupboard and shifted the cereal boxes so she wouldn't see the expression on his face. "Sorry. Is Circe getting picked on now?"

"No. I just wanted some time with her."

"Of course." He straightened up. "I restocked the fridge and the cupboards. I got yogurt and pineapple, and I picked up those cookies—the ones with the jam in the middle." He'd gotten all her favorites, or at least the foods he remembered her liking the last time he'd visited.

The smile on her face was like a breath of fresh air. "Thank you." She put Circe on the ground and went to the fridge, taking out a yogurt. He narrowed his eyes at the chicken, but at least if it took a shit, he wouldn't have to clean it. And if having it around made Etta happy, he would tolerate it.

She sat at the table and peeled the lid off her yogurt. "What happened to your shirt?"

"Hm?" He looked down at the blotchy coffee stain on his sweater and the dried splashes on his jeans. "Oh, I ran into someone at the bakery. It was kind of a mess." He sat at the table beside Etta and tracked the chicken's progress across the floor. It was by Etta's feet now, and it seemed content there. "She said she knows you. Her name's Evvie."

"Mm, yes, I know her." Etta took another bite of yogurt. "She's nice. She volunteers a lot in town, and she used to work at the animal clinic. But she just retired, I think. Like you."

It was odd to think of himself as *retired*, but he supposed he was since the farewell tour was finished. Iridium Twilight was now a thing of the past . . . or it would be, if not for the memoir they were collectively writing.

The thought of writing brought him back to what had happened that morning. "She's also writing a book," he said, and Etta's eyes widened slightly. "A romance."

"Interesting." Etta ate another spoonful of yogurt and stared thoughtfully into the distance. "I didn't know she wrote." She reached down, presumably to pet the chicken. "How did you find out?"

He explained more about the coffee incident and about the one page he'd gotten a glimpse of. "I'm not the best judge, but she seems like a good writer," he said, shrugging.

Etta pushed her empty yogurt container away and reached down, picking up Circe and settling her on her lap. "Are you still struggling with your version of the band's story?" she asked, her head tilted slightly. He knew that look—she had an idea. She looked a bit witchy with her bathrobe on, her graying hair frizzing around her face, and a chicken in her lap.

The mere thought of the memoir made his stress hives flare. "Yes," he mumbled, looking at the table.

She made a thoughtful humming noise. "If Evvie's writing is good, maybe she can help you."

Matthias's head jerked up. "Etta, I don't know about that."

"Why? Evvie is a very nice woman, and I'm sure she'd be happy to help. I have her number somewhere, if you'd like to call her."

This was not at all where he thought this conversation would go. "I don't want to call her," he said. "I barely know her, and I don't want it getting around town that I'm back."

Iridium Twilight was Juniper Creek's claim to fame. Many people around town still knew him even though he hadn't lived there for years. Most of them were nice enough to treat him like the average Joe and let him live peacefully, but he had to be careful. You never knew what people would post online, and when he left LA, he'd looked forward to getting space from all the attention and paparazzi.

If he was being honest with himself, that's partially why he was struggling with the memoir. Why did their private lives need to be on display? Why did people need to know what happened behind the scenes?

"If you ask her to keep it quiet, she will," Etta said.

He wanted to believe her, but it didn't seem like the two women knew each other that well. "I'll think about it," he said, mostly to placate his sister. He had no intention of asking Evvie for help.

"Good. You have to open up to someone at some point, whether that's your fans or someone closer to you."

Not this again. He rolled his eyes. Etta was always getting on his case about his lack of vulnerability, about how he always broke off his relationships because he didn't let people in. But she was never there. She never knew that *he* wasn't the one breaking things off. "This isn't about opening up to someone," he said.

She continued to pet her chicken and shrugged one shoulder at him. "If you say so."

He was tempted to argue, but his phone rang, the ID reading "Bea." He showed the screen to Etta then answered the phone, standing up and going to the window.

"Hey, baby," he said.

"Hey, Dad. Are you at the farm?"

Bea's voice filled him with warmth. Out of his four kids, she was the only one who still talked to him. Although that wasn't really any of their faults.

"Yeah, I am. I got here two days ago." He walked away from Etta and into the living room, just in case Bea asked about her. She'd been the one who suggested he come in the first place; she'd visited Etta last month and had seen how she'd declined. How she was sleeping for longer than usual, how she wasn't eating much or leaving the house.

For all of her adult life, Etta had had persistent depressive disorder. Her antidepressants helped, but they weren't magical pills that created happiness out of the blue. She'd been keeping up with her coping mechanisms until their mother passed away, but that seemed to have triggered another downhill episode. Living alone at the farm couldn't have been good for her, and Bea couldn't visit from Vancouver as often as she wanted.

"You're settling in okay?" Bea asked.

"Yeah. I picked up food today—all of Etta's favorites."

"Aw, you're so sweet, Dad. I know she'll be happier with you there. And, speaking of, I got three weeks off over the holidays! It's practically a miracle. I was thinking maybe I could bring Sophie there and we could spend both Hanukkah and Christmas as a family."

Matthias's heart soared. He hadn't spent the holidays with any of his kids in years, and he hadn't seen his granddaughter Sophie in at least six months. Recording and touring had taken up so much of his time and energy that he hadn't been able to be with his family most of the time. Bea couldn't travel to see him either now because she was a nurse and almost never got time off over the holidays.

"I would love that, Bea! And Etta will too, I know it. We'd love to have you."

"Great!"

The two of them spoke for a few more minutes then hung up. Etta practically glowed when he shared the news that they were going to have family over for both Hanukkah and Christmas.

Matthias wasn't usually a big holiday guy, but Etta had fallen in love with Christmas the first year she'd lived in California. And although he hadn't celebrated many Jewish holidays since he'd left home, it meant a lot to him that he was able to share part of his heritage with his daughter and his granddaughter.

He would embrace every holiday activity this year because he could feel it in his bones: this was going to be the best holiday season he'd ever had.

CHAPTER FIVE

EVVIE

*E*vvie smoothed her leggings and her white sweater as she looked in the mirror, pleased at how the sweater sparkled slightly when she moved. She often braided her long white hair to keep it out of her face, but for this date, Eleanor had shown her how to twist it into a clip so it sat elegantly at the back of her head. Evvie even put on a swipe of pink lip gloss.

That was as dressed up as she was going to get. No shapewear or a full face of makeup for her, no ma'am. She was past caring what others thought about her appearance. After decades of struggling against fatphobia, she'd finally gotten to a place in her sixties where she genuinely loved her body. Not that she didn't have off days, but in general she was fond of her curves and rolls.

If her date wasn't, that would be an easy way to rule him out.

On Evvie's request, they'd agreed to meet at a bistro she liked in Abbotsford. She was familiar with the layout and the menu, so she felt comfortable there. If the date went horribly wrong, at least she would enjoy her meal. And Dylan knew where she was going, so if Evvie went mysteriously missing, Dylan could alert the police.

Her ADHD medication sat on a shelf by the door—so she could easily see it whenever she went out, which helped her remember to take it—but she decided not to take a pill this evening. She might want a drink, and her medication did not mix well with alcohol.

Evvie played another podcast on the way to the bistro—this one about erotica novels. Monster erotica was apparently a popular subgenre, although she hadn't read any yet. The idea of sleeping with an alien or the Mothman admittedly piqued her interest, and she made a mental note to ask Dylan for monster romances when she saw her next.

When she got to the bistro, she gave the host Antonio's name, and the host showed Evvie to a table occupied by one of the handsomest men she had ever seen. He looked even better than he had in his Ember profile photos. His clean-shaven face showed off his square jaw, his white hair was perfectly coiffed, and Evvie was sure his eyebrows must have been professionally shaped. He gazed at her with electric blue eyes, and his white button-up shirt did nothing to hide his well-toned muscles.

He stood to greet her, his grin glaringly white, his teeth perfectly straight. Evvie forced herself to close her open mouth and smile instead of gaping at the man as if he were a zoo animal. "Good evening," he said with a slight accent. His online profile stated he was from Florence but had moved to Canada decades ago. Clearly, his Italian accent had hung on enough to stir something in Evvie's chest. And in other areas.

She cleared her throat. "Hello," she said, reaching out to shake his hand, which was much larger than hers. "You must be Antonio." He gave her that smile again, and her face must have looked like that heart-eyed emoji she often sent Dylan.

"I am. Please sit." He pulled her chair out for her and helped her scooch in. "Was everything alright on the drive over?" he asked as he took his seat across from her.

"Yes, everything was fine. Why?"

"You're five minutes late, that's all," he said, looking at his watch.

"Oh." A tiny alarm bell pinged at the back of Evvie's brain, but she ignored it. This man was charming, so what if he cared that she was a bit late? "Sorry. That tends to be common for me."

He laughed it off. "I hope you don't mind, I ordered us wine already."

As if on cue, their waiter came over and poured the wine, which Antonio swirled around in his glass and sipped, his eyebrows drawing together as he made his judgement. "It'll do."

They spoke a bit about the weather, wondering whether it would snow this year, then Evvie realized there were no menus on the table. She already knew her favorite dishes at the bistro, but she enjoyed asking each waiter for their recommendations. "Where are the menus?" she asked.

"Ah," he said, rolling up his pristine white sleeves. "I took the liberty of ordering for us."

"Oh. Okay." Another alarm bell, but it was difficult for Evvie to notice when her focus was on Antonio's rather firm-looking forearms. "Wh-what did you order for me?" she said, trying her best to look at his eyes.

But those were just as mesmerizing, and staring into them made it difficult to absorb what he was saying. "I ordered a steak for myself—rare, of course. And for you, the salmon."

"Salmon?" She wasn't big on sea food, but if she had to pick a fish to eat, salmon wasn't the worst.

"Yes, it's healthy," he said.

The glint in his eye took on a distinctly darker tone. What had started out as thoughtfulness veered into less savory territory. Evvie squirmed in her seat. She needed to pull the conversation back into her side of the court.

"So, on your profile it says you spend your weekends looking for deer," she started. That was a safe point to connect on. Evvie loved animals, after all.

"I do," he answered, taking a sip of wine. The way he looked at her as his lips touched the glass made it difficult to notice anything but his mouth. Those *lips*.

"Um, do you like any other animals? I worked at a vet clinic before I retired, and I'm fond of dogs of any kind."

"Dogs?" He leaned back and laughed as if she'd told the world's funniest joke.

Confused, she responded with a forced "Ha ha."

"I don't like pets," he said once he'd stopped guffawing. "They make a mess, and they restrict one's freedom. I look for deer because I *hunt* them. Deer, moose, bear. Foxes, sometimes. And I fish. There's a lake about forty minutes from here, best fish you'll ever catch . . ."

As Antonio talked about fishing and recounted the last hunting trip he'd been on with his sons, the glow that had framed him when she walked in dimmed considerably. He was still talking as the waiter brought their food, and Evvie could barely get a word in edgewise. She settled for taking bites of her salmon and the side of veggies he'd ordered for her—veggies!—as he continued to talk, eating his steak at the same time and barely chewing before he swallowed.

Evvie poured herself more wine, and her thoughts drifted to the man she'd crashed into at the bakery on Monday. She wondered if he liked animals; he must, since he grew up on a farm. He'd at least have more respect for them than Antonio did, most likely. Antonio talked about hunting and fishing as if they were games and the animals didn't matter. He even lowered his voice at one point and leaned in to tell her how she could get around the hunting quotas if she was careful.

By the time she'd finished her meal, the alarm bells in her head were one long blaring siren. Finishing her wine, she scooched her chair out and grabbed her jacket. Antonio stopped talking in the middle of a sentence and raised his brows. "Where are you going? We haven't had dessert yet."

She tried her darnedest not to roll her eyes as she slung her purse over her shoulder. "Listen, Antonio, I don't think this is going to work. Thank you for dinner, but I'm not interested in dessert." Or anything else, for that matter.

"Wait," he said, getting up and moving to stand in front of her. "Are you sure you want to go? I had a surprise for you after dinner."

She stepped back and crossed her arms. It would take one heck of a surprise to salvage this dumpster fire of a date. "Oh?"

He leaned toward her, bringing his mouth closer to her ear than she was comfortable with. "I have a friend at home," he said softly. "I thought you might want to meet her."

Evvie inhaled sharply and took a much larger step back than she had before. "Excuse me?" Why would he think she was at all interested in a threesome? And with *him*, of all people?

He was still smiling, as if she'd played a good trick on him. When she didn't move and continued to glare, he said, "On your profile. On Ember. It says you're bisexual?"

She blew out a breath. "*Bisexual*. Not *polyamorous*. Not *a swinger*. Not *looking for a threesome*."

His frown was genuine now. "But you're bisexual." He said it like it was the most straightforward thing in the world, like being bisexual obviously made her open to threesomes.

She laughed, her hand in front of her mouth. "Antonio, honey, let me tell you something. You need to learn to respect other people. Do some research about bisexuality, okay?" She moved around him, heading for the door, then paused and looked back. He was watching her, shaking his head as if *she* had done something wrong. "Also, don't order food for other people. It's rude. And maybe have an actual conversation with your date instead of monologuing. You might have more success that way."

She spun on her heel and continued to walk away, but he called after her, "Well, you won't have *any* success looking like that."

Closing her eyes, she took a deep breath and kept going. He wasn't worth it.

Maybe trying to date again wasn't worth the headache.

～

EVVIE'S LOW was the talk of the evening at the next queer seniors' group meeting. After she finished relaying the whole story about Antonio and his misogynistic ways, Priya squeezed her hand.

"I am so sorry," she said.

Gem gave her a hug, then took her seat again. "Men can be such assholes."

"They really can be," Noah said, shaking his head. "I can't believe he said that to you. That he said all of that to you, and that he treated you that way!" He gagged. "Sorry, I can't stand people like that."

"Are you okay?" Tom asked him.

"Yes, love, just upset for Evvie," Noah said, patting Tom's knee.

Tom looked at Evvie, his brow wrinkled in concern. "Oh no, what happened?"

It wasn't unusual for Tom to forget things people had said five minutes ago. Usually, Evvie wouldn't have minded repeating herself, but she really didn't want to relive the date again. She smiled at Noah in relief when he said, "I'll tell you later, babe," and rubbed Tom's arm.

"I deleted the app when I got home," Evvie told them, avoiding Priya's gaze. "I don't think the dating game is for me anymore." Not if she'd have to sift through people like Antonio to find someone kind and trustworthy.

"Oh, love, don't say that," Priya said, still holding Evvie's hand. "There's someone out there for you. Maybe try . . . not a man, next time?"

Gem, Noah, and Evvie laughed, but something in Evvie's chest constricted. She had felt uneasy before her date with Antonio because she was going on a date with a man. She'd been married to a man once, and that relationship had imploded thanks to her cheating husband, Simon. But even before he cheated, she'd felt insecure at being with a man.

She'd known she was queer since high school, and it hadn't

made much of a difference in her life until she'd met a few queer friends right after she graduated. She'd avoided telling them about Simon because some of them would have accused her of not being queer enough; she'd seen them react that way to others. When she and Simon got married, she drifted apart from those friends and hadn't heard from them since.

Even though Priya meant well with her comment, she'd poked at the bruise Evvie still carried, the one that never fully went away. The one that told her maybe she shouldn't be in the queer group in the first place because she'd never had a serious relationship with a woman.

All she said in response was, "Maybe." When Gem pulled out a game of Phase 10 for them all to play, she wanted to hug her friend, relieved that everyone's attention went to something other than her dating life.

Ember had been a failed experiment, a research trip gone wrong, and the thought of organizing a date with someone else gave Evvie the heebie-jeebies. Antonio had reminded her how vulnerable romantic relationships were, and she wasn't ready to put herself in someone else's hands to that extent again. Romance just wasn't for her anymore, and it looked like she wouldn't be applying her own experience to her novel any time soon. Being the third—or fifth—wheel and continuing to inhale romance novels seemed like her only options.

Either that, or give up on her book altogether. Maybe she wasn't meant to be an author either. How could someone who had given up on romance write anything meaningful about that very subject?

CHAPTER SIX

MATTHIAS

*M*atthias hadn't been able to get Etta to leave the house once since he'd arrived, and he didn't know how she was avoiding cabin fever. As far as he could tell, she spent most of her time taking care of her chickens, sketching, or doing needlepoint. It was all so quiet, so insular. Just watching her made him feel lonely.

Iridium Twilight's farewell tour had been over for a month, but at least in LA he'd had friends to meet with for lunch and coffee. He'd had events to go to, fellow musicians to support.

Here, there was nothing. Just him and Etta. He couldn't wait until Bea and Sophie arrived so they'd have an excuse to do things and go places.

That didn't solve the problem of getting Etta out, though. She'd feel better once she did, but getting her to leave her comfortable routine was nearly impossible.

He'd been into town twice since the incident at the bakery on Monday. Once to pick up supplies to help Etta fix the chicken coop, and a second time just to see how Juniper Creek had changed. It hadn't much. Like this time of year when he was a kid, the town was covered in holiday decor: snowflake decals on windows, Christmas lights on awnings, and wreaths and red ribbons on streetlamps. The bookshop displayed holiday romances at the front, and a decorated Christmas tree stood in front of the library. There were even flyers posted around town already for Creekfest, Juniper Creek's New Year's Eve celebration.

Matthias had kept his head down and avoided making eye contact with people for the most part, just in case. Júlian Flores had recognized him at the hardware store; they'd gone to school together and kept in touch enough for a brief conversation. There was little chance Júlian would post anything about him on social media, though.

Since Matthias's knee was feeling better, he'd walked around the pond, his hood pulled up against the rain, and then headed to the bakery again for a warm drink. When he was growing up, a white couple had owned the bakery—an intimidating man with a gold front tooth and his wife. The owners now were Indian, if Matthias guessed correctly, and half the display case was filled with desserts he'd never tried. He was determined to taste each of them while he was in town.

An unexpected wave of disappointment had washed over him when he opened the bakery door and saw only one other customer inside—a customer who wasn't Evvie. He found himself wondering about her more than once during the week. Did she re-print her manuscript pages? How was the editing going? What was her novel about? He blamed Etta for these thoughts since she had suggested he ask Evvie for help. And his own writing was going dismally. Meaning he hadn't started yet.

Instead of working on the memoir, he'd been researching what he could do around the house to brighten Etta's days. He found a site about joyful little things to make a space cozier and happier, and he'd made a list of items to buy that he thought Etta would like.

He was going into town again now to find some of those items. "Etta, I'm going out for a bit," he called. When she didn't respond, he went to her room to find her curled up on her bed, asleep. He gently pulled her lilac-colored blanket over her and backed out of the room quietly, then wrote a note about where he was going and stuck it to her doorframe.

Just as he got in the car, his phone rang. "Hey, Nick," he answered.

"Matthias, buddy! How're things in the Great White North?" Nick was yelling, and there were multiple other voices in the background.

"Where are you?" Matthias asked, holding the phone away from his ear. "It's loud."

The voices on the other end suddenly quieted, and when Nick spoke again, it was at a normal volume. "Yeah, sorry. I'm out with the boys." Of course he was. Matthias suppressed a sigh. "How's Loretta?"

"She's okay." The longer Mattias stayed with her, the more he saw what Bea had talked about—the listlessness, the lack of motivation, the food avoidance. But he wasn't about to tell Nick all that. "I'm actually heading out now to get some things for her."

"Look at you, such a sweet big brother," Nick said. It was a bit of a dig, but Matthias heard the sincerity in his voice too. "Have you started your part of the story yet?"

There it was. The *real* reason Nick had called, most likely.

"Yeah, yeah," Matthias replied. "I have. It's coming along well."

"Awesome, man, that's great to hear. I'd love to read it, but Colin doesn't want us exchanging stories in case we influence each other. He says it will be more authentic if we don't know each other's perspectives."

Colin had a point, and Matthias was grateful for it because he didn't have to make up an excuse about why he had nothing to show Nick.

"Right, right, yeah."

"Okay, well, I gotta go, but we'll talk later, right? Give Loretta a kiss for me." And with that, Nick was gone.

There was no way Matthias was going to follow up on that request. Nick had had a thing for Etta once upon a time, and

Matthias had popped his bubble by revealing she was lesbian. "Being gay must run in the family, hey?" Nick had said, and Matthias had rolled his eyes, not bothering to explain that liking men didn't make him gay since he also liked women. Matthias's revelation didn't stop Nick from flirting with Etta, though, and she complained about how annoying Nick was whenever they were in the same city.

Matthias couldn't blame her, really. Nick was an acquired taste, even as a best friend, and even if he meant well.

Matthias took his time in town, soaking up the fresh air outside, even though it was chilly and humid. He'd found Juniper Creek boring when he was younger, but now it was a nice change to the bustle and vastness of LA.

By the time he'd found most of the items on his list, his knee was aching and his energy was flagging. He drove toward the diner to get himself lunch, feeling slightly guilty that he was eating without Etta. The inside of The June Bug diner was festive with white-lit garlands hanging on the walls and snowman figurines on the booth dividers. He spotted a menorah and a kinara as well, which was impressive for a town this small; he hadn't expected to see anything outside of Christmas decor.

Someone had left a newspaper on the table where he sat, so he flipped through it as he ate. One of the articles caught his eye. He snapped a photo of it and sent it to Etta. If anything could get her out of the house, this could.

"Excuse me," said someone at his elbow. It was one of the teenagers who worked at the diner. "Are you Matthias Vogel from Iridium Twilight?"

Shit. A teenager was sure to post about this on social media, and the paparazzi would come running. Matthias forced his shoulders to stay relaxed. "No, sorry, kid. I've got that a couple of times, though. Whoever he is, he must be good looking." So much for having a quiet lunch. Once the teen was gone, Matthias inhaled his food and headed home.

~

"I CAN'T BELIEVE we're going skating," Etta said as Matthias put her skates in the trunk of his car on Saturday. "I haven't been skating in years. What if I can't remember how?"

"*You're* going skating," he corrected her. "If I tried, I'd be flat on my ass in seconds." Just thinking about skating made his knee throb. "And you'll remember. You might be a bit shaky at first, but it's like riding a bike, isn't it? You were in lessons for what . . . fifteen years? Your muscles will remember even if you don't."

"I hope you're right."

"You can always use one of those ice walker trainers if you need to."

She snorted. "Over my dead body. If I can't hold myself up without one, we're leaving."

"Fair enough."

The parking lot at the rink in Chilliwack was more crowded than Matthias had expected, and inside was just as busy. There were a few kids on the ice and some younger people, but most of the skaters looked over sixty, which made sense since anyone aged sixty-five or over could skate for free today.

Matthias helped Etta put her skates on. She wrung her hands as she watched the other skaters. As far as Matthias could tell, none of them were particularly elegant; most of them shuffled around with the walker trainers just as they'd move with a walker off the ice.

"You'll be fine," he said, grasping his sister's hands. "Didn't you used to say you felt like your best self on the ice?"

Etta pulled her hair back and secured it with an elastic. "Yes, I did, but that was more than four decades ago. I'm not exactly a spring chicken anymore. Where will you be sitting?"

Matthias spotted an empty space nearby in the stands, right by the boards. "There. I'll be as close to the ice as I can get, just in case." And so he didn't have to walk up the stairs.

"Okay."

She clung to his arm as she hobbled over to the ice, and her eyes widened as she stepped onto the slippery surface. She smiled at him hesitantly and grabbed the board nearest to her as she let go of his hand. He stayed there for a few moments until she worked up the confidence to push off the board. She wobbled a bit but kept going.

Once he was sure she wouldn't fall, he went to sit on the bottom row of bleachers, where he'd told Etta he would. He kept an eye on her, a smile growing on his face the longer he watched. It took her a couple laps around the rink, but he could pinpoint the moment she decided her legs were still strong enough to carry her. She picked up speed, her movements becoming smoother, more graceful. She even did a twirl at one point and waved at him, laughing, her cheeks tinged pink. He laughed as well and waved back.

Skating was definitely a good idea.

His phone vibrated in his pocket, so he checked it to see that Nick had linked an article in the band's group chat. The headline stated "Nick Evans Crashes Car to Save Ducks."

"What the hell?" Matthias read through the article, and it recounted exactly what the headline advertised. Nick had been in a car crash—he was clearly fine since he was the one who sent the article—because he'd swerved to avoid hitting two ducks. His car was totaled, but according to the text, he sustained only "minor injuries."

Matthias dialed Nick's number, glancing at Etta again as he did so. "Hey, Matty," Nick answered, sounding cheery.

"You crashed your car?"

"Yeah." Nick laughed. "I'm fine, though. And I saved the ducks! They were right in the middle of the road, I swear. Just hanging out, doing their ducky thing."

Matthias shook his head. "How did you not see these ducks in time to stop?"

"That's the thing. The officer wouldn't give my license back until I saw an optometrist. So I can't drive again until after my appointment, as long as I can actually see fine." He didn't sound particularly worried.

"How've you been getting around then?"

"I've been driving him," said another voice. Steven, of course —their bass player. "He's staying in the guest room for now." Steven didn't take any shit from Nick. He was the youngest in the band, but he acted like an older brother to Nick and Matthias.

"Ah." Matthias got caught up in talking to the two of them, and by the time he hung up, he'd lost track of Etta.

When he finally spotted her, she was skating slowly with a group of women, three of them using the skate trainers and two of them skating freely. The group of six moved around the rink in a little clump, other people skating around them.

Etta was leaning closer to one of the ladies skating freely who wore a bright pink jacket and a rainbow scarf, her white hair braided down her back. She looked familiar somehow . . . As they skated closer and her features became clearer, it hit Matthias where he knew her from. It was Evvie from the bakery. Her jacket was clean now, and her hair had been down the last time he saw her. Two of the other ladies looked familiar as well. He was sure they each owned one of the two flower shops in Juniper Creek.

What was Etta talking to Evvie about? Evvie nodded, and Etta pointed in his direction. Matthias groaned. Was she asking Evvie to help him with the book? He hadn't wanted people knowing who he was yet. Or ever, really. Sure, he missed the number of activities available to him constantly in LA, but he did not miss the swarms of fans and paparazzi.

He didn't know how Nick could stand it; being the lead singer, he was under way more scrutiny than Matthias or Steven. Nick was a different person, though. He seemed to thrive in the limelight, and even Steven didn't seem to mind it much. But Matthias wasn't like that, and every time he went out with the guys, he had to prepare himself for anything.

And now Etta was blowing his cover.

He slouched in his seat and tried to focus on the rest of the article, but his mind was elsewhere now. A spot on the back of his arm started to itch—his stress hives, back with a vengeance.

"Matthias." He looked up to see Etta standing at the boards in front of him—with Evvie. A grin spread across Etta's face. "Look who I found."

CHAPTER SEVEN

EVVIE

*W*hen Evvie had found out the arena in Chilliwack was having a free seniors' skate day on Saturday, she'd rounded up her friends. If she couldn't find a date to enjoy the holiday season with, she'd make her own fun. Even if she was a fifth wheel, yet again.

Eleanor had been on board right away, of course, which meant Minnie was also going to come.

When Evvie had shown up at the library to convince Dylan to join them, Frankie had been there too, editing photos at one of the tables. After Evvie had explained her skating-day plan, Dylan had scowled.

"I'm going to fall on my ass. I haven't skated in years, and even when I did, I couldn't figure out how to stop properly."

Evvie shook her head. "You'll be fine. They have skate trainers you can hold on to so you won't fall."

Dylan looked even more horrified. "You want me to use a skate trainer?"

"I don't think you'd be the only one." Frankie smoothed her hand up and down Dylan's arm. "It is seniors' skate day, after all."

"Thank you, Frankie," Evvie said. "See? It'll be fun. Please?"

Dylan practically growled as she turned to look at Frankie. "Do you want to go?"

Frankie hesitated, then said, "It could be fun. I'll even leave my camera at home so there won't be any evidence if you do fall on your ass."

Rolling her eyes, Dylan said, "Fine. We'll go."

Until they were on the ice, Evvie had spent every minute worrying that Dylan would back out, but Frankie's enthusiasm must have helped because all five of them were on the ice now, and Evvie felt like she could fly. Even though she was skating quite slowly.

Minnie, Frankie, and Dylan were all using the skate trainers. Eleanor had started with one but had gotten rid of it after a few laps. Evvie herself was a bit wobbly at first, but she'd been skating quite often throughout her life—winter was her favorite season, after all—and she relished the power in her legs and the breeze that caressed her face. The Christmas carols playing on the speakers overhead rounded out the festive atmosphere nicely, and everyone seemed to be enjoying themselves. Dylan had stopped grumbling, at least.

"My goodness, is that how old we look?" Minnie asked, gaping at two women also using skate trainers across the rink.

Frankie stifled a laugh, and before anyone could answer, someone skated up to Evvie, catching her arm. The two of them teetered. "Sorry, Evvie, I meant that to be a softer landing."

"Loretta! How are you?" She hadn't seen Loretta in a few months, at least. Her face was thinner than Evvie remembered, but her cheeks had a healthy glow.

"I'm good, I'm good. How are you? My brother ran into you in town the other day. He said you're writing a book!"

Evvie gaped like a fish for a moment, then remembered her run-in with the man at the bakery. Of course he'd told his sister about her manuscript. "Matthias, right?" she said, avoiding the topic of her book. "I didn't know you had a brother until he mentioned you."

The two of them began to skate side by side, keeping up with the others.

"Yes, that's him. He was very sorry about spilling coffee on your papers."

"That's alright," Evvie said, brushing it off. "They weren't important. So . . . is he visiting for the holidays?"

Loretta sighed. "Not exactly. I think he's here to take care of me, to be honest. I don't need a babysitter, but here we are." She rolled her eyes. "It is nice to have company, though. My niece and her daughter are coming in a few weeks for the holidays, so I'll have a full house for once!"

They talked about the farm and the chickens, then Loretta said, "Listen, I've got a favor to ask."

A tightness blossomed beneath Evvie's sternum. She wasn't the best at saying no, which is why she ended up volunteering for so many events in Juniper Creek. It's not that she didn't enjoy them, but sometimes she wanted to participate as an attendee, not as a volunteer. "A favor?"

"It's writing related. My brother has a . . . project on the go that needs to be finished by the first of January. But he's struggling with it. He's not much of a writer, and he doesn't know how to get his thoughts organized. I thought, since you're writing a novel, you might be able to help him."

Evvie almost laughed. Organizing thoughts of any kind was not on her list of skills. In fact, it was on the list of whatever the opposite of skills was. Flaws? Failures? Ineptitudes? "I'm not sure I'd be the best person to help him."

"Oh, I'm sure it'd be fine. Honestly, I think he just needs to get started. And he won't let just anyone help him. It has to be someone he trusts."

Evvie frowned. "And he trusts me? We just met. Once. When we spilled coffee on each other."

"I think he'll trust you once he gets to know you. He's over there." She pointed to the stands, but Evvie couldn't see Matthias.

"Why don't we go over and have a chat with him? Just to see what he thinks. If you're willing to help, that is."

Part of Evvie wanted to say no, but a bigger part of her was curious. What was Matthias writing? If it was fiction, maybe she *could* help. She'd gone through a phase of wanting to be an author in her thirties—which is when she'd written her story—and she'd been studying writing again since she found the handwritten pages. She also knew the value of privacy and respecting an author's work; putting writing out into the world was one of the most vulnerable things a person could do. At the very least, the two of them could be accountability buddies.

It helped that Matthias was easy on the eyes.

"Sure, why not?" Evvie said. She told the others to keep skating, then let Loretta lead her to the sideboards.

As they got closer, she spotted Matthias in the bottom row of the stands. His head was down, but she recognized his hair and his lanky build. He didn't seem the most comfortable, sitting hunched on the bench with his cane leaning next to him.

"Matthias," Loretta said. He looked up at them, his brown eyes locking with Evvie's. "Look who I found."

Evvie had the fleeting thought that the feeling in her stomach was the one she'd been looking for on her date with Antonio. *This* was what she wanted to describe in her novel. *This* was what the heroine would feel when she saw her love interest for the first time.

Pushing that thought aside, Evvie smiled. "Hello."

"Evvie, hey," Matthias said. His voice seemed extra gruff, and he cleared his throat. "How are you? Did you get your manuscript re-printed?"

"I did, thank you. And I'm doing well."

"So . . ." Loretta looked back and forth between them. "Matthias, I told Evvie about your project." He looked as if he was about to scold her, but she held up her hand. "I didn't say what it was about, just that you needed help with a writing project. And if you're open to it, Evvie is willing to help."

Matthias pursed his lips, and Evvie could practically feel the tension rolling off him. This seemed like a conversation she shouldn't be present for; what if he said yes just because he couldn't say no in front of her? That was something she would do. She didn't want to force him into anything he didn't want.

"Why don't we meet for coffee and talk about the project first?" she suggested. "That way, I can see if I'll actually be helpful, and you can decide if you actually want my help." She'd be thinking about the meeting every second leading up to it, but this was a more casual and flexible option for them both.

He raised his eyebrows. "That's not a bad idea. Let's do that. Although, let's not spill coffee on each other this time."

Evvie laughed, shielding her mouth with her hand. "Deal."

"Perfect," Loretta said. "Shall we skate some more, Evvie?"

They waited for Minnie, Eleanor, Dylan, and Frankie to come back around, then they rejoined the group. As Evvie skated, she couldn't help but glance over at Matthias periodically, and more than once, she swore he was also looking at her.

SUNDAY EVENING, Evvie and Frankie stood at Evvie's stove, cooking butter chicken for the weekly dinner Evvie hosted for her friends. Dylan and Minnie sat at the table, but Eleanor had been unable to make this dinner because of a staff meeting at her flower shop. While Evvie missed her, it did free up some room in her tiny kitchen.

"So you're going to help Matthias with his writing? Like a tutor?" Minnie asked.

On the ride home from the rink the day before, Evvie had told Dylan and Frankie about her conversation with Matthias and Loretta. Dylan had just about crashed the car when Evvie said Matthias's name. "Loretta's brother . . . Matthias Vogel?" Her eyes widened comically. "The drummer from Iridium Twilight?"

"Maybe?" Evvie asked.

"It's him, for sure. You realize he's famous, right? They just got off their farewell tour!" Dylan wasn't a jump-up-and-down kind of person, but it seemed like she would have done that very action if she hadn't been driving.

"That must be why he looked familiar," Evvie had mused. She enjoyed listening to music, but she'd never been the type of person to know musicians' names or follow their lives in the media.

Dylan had pursed her lips as if she were in pain at Evvie's lack of excitement, and for the rest of the drive, she'd held herself with a sense of restraint.

Now Evvie was filling in Minnie, who had driven home with Eleanor.

"I'm not sure exactly how I'll be helping yet," Evvie said, stirring the butter chicken. Frankie was rolling out the naan on the counter, which Evvie had finished prepping just as her friends arrived. "I'm going to Loretta's for coffee tomorrow, so I'll find out then."

"Matthias Vogel!" Dylan blurted, obviously still starstruck. "Do you think you could get an autograph for me?"

Evvie laughed. "Sure, I'll try."

Frankie turned abruptly and looked at Minnie. "Are you alright?"

"Hm?" Minnie blinked at Frankie as if she'd been lost in thought.

"You've been fidgeting since you got here. I haven't known you for long, but that doesn't seem like something you do often."

Evvie wished she had Frankie's ability to notice things like that; she hadn't noticed Minnie fidgeting. But she supposed being observant came with the territory of photography. And anyway, she'd been focused on making dinner.

Minnie bit her lip. "Well, I'm kind of nervous. I want to ask you all for a favor."

Another favor? Well, at least people were giving Evvie something to do with her time.

Minnie took a deep breath, all eyes on her. "You know that Eleanor moved into my place a couple weeks ago."

They all nodded. Evvie had been over the moon when Eleanor had told her she was moving into Minnie's house. They'd only been a couple since August, but anyone who saw them together knew they were meant to be. Even Dylan, who was cynical about love—although less so since Frankie had moved in with her.

Evvie couldn't help the jealousy crawling up her throat, trying to make her unhappy for her friends. Why had they all found love in the past few months, but she hadn't? Why had her attempt at dating gone sour?

"It might seem like we're moving fast, but we're not getting any younger, so . . ." Minnie sat up straighter and pushed her shoulders back. "I'm going to ask her to marry me."

Evvie squealed and dropped the wooden spoon into the butter chicken, splashing tomato sauce on her shirt. Frankie gasped, and Dylan's jaw dropped.

"Oh, Minnie!" Evvie brushed the sauce off her shirt with a cloth, then threw her arms around Minnie's shoulders. "This is so exciting!"

Minnie laughed, her face red. "It is, but you can't tell her, okay? I want your help." She looked around at them all. "You know what Eleanor is like. She deserves the world, and I want the proposal to be perfect and magical, just like she is."

"Of course we'll help," Evvie said, feeling like she was about to burst into a shower of sparkles.

"I can capture the whole thing on camera," Frankie said, her eyes bright.

Dylan nodded. "Whatever you need, we're here for you."

The rest of the evening was full of brainstorming and planning. They didn't settle on anything concrete, but Minnie seemed to have an idea of how she wanted everything to work. The one thing set in stone was that she'd propose on the winter solstice, which Eleanor celebrated instead of Christmas. Evvie could barely contain her excitement, and somehow she'd have to hide it from Eleanor.

As her friends left for the evening and she waved goodbye to them, the bubbly feeling inside her turned heavy. She closed the door and swallowed thickly, rubbing her chest. The feeling worked its way up into her throat, and before she knew it, she was crying.

She collapsed on her couch, her head in her hands. She wanted to be so happy for Minnie and Eleanor—she *was* happy for them—but they were getting everything she wanted. Everything she told herself she was fine without.

Now that she was retired and she had no work to consume her—no clear purpose, and way too much time to think—she felt the ache of being alone. Of not having someone to cuddle with at night, to wake up with in the morning, to go on cute dates with. She let herself sob for a few minutes, then she pulled herself together.

She *did* have a purpose. She would write her novel, putting everything on the page that she wished for in a relationship. And she would do anything she could to make Minnie's proposal the most magical moment Juniper Creek had ever seen.

CHAPTER EIGHT

MATTHIAS

*M*atthias hadn't had a chance to set up his furniture purchases on Saturday morning—in other words, he'd slept in—and the same thing happened on Sunday. With his career as a musician, he'd reliably become a night owl. So he waited until Etta went to bed on Sunday night, then began his work. He wanted her to see the house transformed in the morning, hoping it would give her a serotonin boost for the day.

It didn't hurt that Evvie was coming for coffee on Monday afternoon, so the house would look extra homey for her visit. Not that he cared what she thought.

First up: the lighting. It made sense that more light would chase away the darkness of depression. As quietly as he could, Matthias took down the black-out curtains in the living room and replaced them with sheer yellow ones. He'd read that yellow was proven to lift spirits and brighten the room, and sunlight could filter through these much better than through the heavy old fabric. He also took down the bent blinds in the kitchen, replacing them with gauzy white curtains. Let there be light!

The rest of his tasks were easier. In the living room, he set up a wooden bookshelf he'd bought from an antique store and shifted the coffee table books into it, along with a few of the ornaments that had been sitting around the TV. When they set up for Hanukkah, he would replace the ornaments with the menorah. Less clutter, more peace of mind.

On top of the bookshelf, he rested a tall rectangular mirror to create the illusion of the space being bigger and more open—less confining. On the middle shelf, he placed a diffuser he'd bought—from a flower shop, of all places—then filled it with lavender essential oil and plugged it in. Then he padded back and forth from his room, bringing out the plants he'd bought in their quirky pots. He'd never been a plant person, but Eleanor, the shop's owner, had been more than helpful. With her guidance, he'd gotten two spider plants, a string of pearls, a large monstera, and a hedgehog aloe. Once he was happy with the plant arrangement, he hauled out the weighted blanket he'd ordered online before he arrived and folded it neatly on the couch.

Now he had only one thing left to do. Well, two. The next day a worker from the hardware store was coming out to put up the lights outside. Matthias wasn't about to climb a ladder, so hiring help was a no-brainer. He wasn't the smartest man, but he knew his limits. Not to mention his bad knee.

It was a good thing Etta was a deep sleeper, because he had to hammer a nail into the wall above the fireplace to hang the circular painting he'd bought from the gallery. A couple of whacks with the hammer, and it was done. He stood there for a moment, cringing and listening for any movement from Etta's room, but there was nothing. He breathed a sigh of relief and hung the painting.

If he were buying something for himself, he would have gone with brighter colors, maybe something red and orange. Something bold. But Etta was a more subtle person. She wore muted colors and the furniture she bought was gray or a soft brown, which was why he'd settled on an abstract green and yellow painting. There was no real picture there, but the swirls and splatters were interesting. He'd find out the next day whether he'd made the right choice.

He called it a night after that. For once he fell asleep easily, satisfied with his work.

∽

He tried not to hold his breath as he walked out to the kitchen late the next morning. He hadn't heard any sounds, which wasn't unusual; Etta was probably out feeding the chickens and cleaning their coop, like she did every morning.

She wasn't, though. She was sitting on the couch, curled up under the weighted blanket, the new curtains wide open and natural light filling the room. He stopped in the doorway, and she looked at him, her eyes glistening and a smile on her face.

"Come here," she said.

"Okay." He walked over to her and she patted the couch by her feet, so he sat.

The second his butt touched the cushion, she reached over and squeezed his arm. "What is all of this?"

"Do you like it?"

"Do I like it?" She rolled her eyes. "I love it. I didn't know this space needed sprucing up, but apparently it did."

He sat taller. "I'm glad."

"You have to water the plants, though," she said. "I can be trusted with animals, not green things."

He laughed. "I'll water the plants."

"And, Matthias . . ." Her gaze was fond, but also slightly exasperated. "You know you can't *cure* my depression, right? All of this"—she gestured around the room—"might help, but it won't make it go away."

"I know." He gripped her hand. "But it can make the days easier, right?"

"Maybe."

He ruffled her hair, and she swatted him away. "Would you like breakfast?"

"I ate already. Cereal. One of the new ones you got, with the cranberries. And I made a pot of coffee."

"Oh, thanks." He got up and grabbed two cups, then returned and handed her one.

"You're spoiling me," she said, leaning against the armrest.

"You can pay me back when my knee goes out and you have to wheel me around."

She rolled her eyes again.

The two of them sat on the couch together, Matthias enjoying his coffee and Etta staring out the window, looking as serene as he'd ever seen her.

When he got up for a bowl of cereal, she said, "Evvie is coming over this afternoon, right?"

"Yeah. Why?"

"Are you prepared?"

He paused, the milk jug poised over his bowl. "Prepared for what?"

"To tell her about the project. Do you know what you need help with?"

"Ha." His cereal ready, he returned the milk to the fridge and went to sit beside her again. "I need help with *all of it*. I have no idea what I'm doing."

"Hm. Maybe don't tell her that. You might scare her off."

He didn't want to scare her off, but he didn't know how she could help him either. "This was your idea," he said around a mouthful of Cheerios. "Maybe you should stay for the conversation."

She shook her head. "This is your problem. You figure it out. I'm going to shower." Without another word, she left him on the couch with his cereal and his problems. And his stress hives, which she had a talent for aggravating.

Evvie would be there in four hours.

He groaned. Was he supposed to put together a job posting for this? A list of responsibilities? Wasn't this just a friend helping a friend? He wasn't even Evvie's friend, really, just an acquaintance who'd spilled coffee on her.

Leaning his head on the back of the couch, he stared at the ceiling. Only he would need help asking for help.

Sitting there with no ideas wasn't doing him any favors, so he went to his room to get ready for the day. The guy he'd hired would be there soon to put up the lights, and Matthias would need to show him exactly what he wanted. He focused on that task, pushing Evvie to the back of his mind.

Four hours. He'd figure out something.

CHAPTER NINE

EVVIE

*C*offee with Matthias wasn't until two o'clock that afternoon. Evvie probably could have worked on her knitting or made cookies in the morning, but she felt like she didn't have enough time to jump into an activity. She was stuck in the limbo of waiting, of knowing she had somewhere to be and something to do later, which made it impossible to get anything else done.

She told herself she had plenty of time and lazed about in her pajamas, trying to read but not absorbing any of the story. Eventually, she gave up and got ready, putting on her bright blue sweater and sparkly white leggings. She put in her dangling snowflake earrings for a nice wintery touch—even though there wasn't any snow yet—and braided her hair over her shoulder.

There would be snow soon, she hoped. It wouldn't be a real winter without snow.

She drove to the library and invited Dylan to lunch. Frankie met them at the diner; she'd also recently retired and had lots of free time on her hands.

"Excited for your coffee date?" Dylan asked as they dug in to their burgers. "I can't believe you'll be spending time with *Matthias Vogel*."

"It's not a date," Evvie said, popping a fry into her mouth. "I'm just helping him with his story." Dylan and Frankie shared a look. It would have been cute if it hadn't been about Evvie. "What?" she asked.

Frankie shrugged. "You said he's handsome, right? I wouldn't blame you if you had something more than writing in mind."

Evvie scowled at her. "I don't." After the disaster with Antonio, she wasn't keen on dating. But she still needed to research romance for her novel.

"There's a winter market on Wednesday in Abbotsford," she said firmly, trying to hint at her friends to drop the dating subject. If she left space in the Matthias conversation, Dylan would want to talk about Iridium Twilight yet again. "Would one of you be able to come with me? Or both of you even?" Markets seemed like a great place for romance novel research. Couples went on dates there all the time, right?

"Ah." Dylan swallowed and took a sip of her water. "Frankie and I are busy on Wednesday, actually."

Frankie nodded. "We're staying with my brother in Vancouver to celebrate American Thanksgiving. Plus, they're going to Hawaii for Christmas, so we're going to celebrate that early. Two holidays in one!"

"I told you yesterday. Remember, Ev?" Dylan added.

"Oh, right. Okay." She didn't remember, but that was nothing new. If she didn't set a reminder in her phone for events, she often forgot about them. In any case, she had other friends she could ask to go with her, so it wasn't the end of the world that Dylan and Frankie were busy.

But when she went to Thistles and Stems after lunch to ask Eleanor, her friend said, "Minnie and I are both working on Wednesday. I'm sorry, dearie."

Evvie sighed, but she understood. It was the slowest season for florists, and it was more cost effective for Minnie and Eleanor to run their own stores rather than bringing in their employees.

There was one more thing she could try. She messaged the

Abbotsford LGBTQ+ Seniors Facebook group, the one Gem had set up so they could stay in touch and keep track of the snack schedule. The chances of one of her seniors' group friends being available was high since all of them were retired and they all lived in Abbotsford.

But within fifteen minutes, everyone had turned her down. Noah said Tom wasn't having a good week, Gem was going to see a movie with Margie, and Priya was visiting her sister on Wednesday.

Why did everyone have something to do—and someone to do it with—except for Evvie? It wasn't any of their faults, really, but it upset her nonetheless. She wasn't about to go to the market by herself. A solo trip did not constitute research for a romance story. She needed interaction, camaraderie, even if it was platonic. She needed to *feel* something so she could translate it to the page.

To lift her mood, she went to Yellow Brick Books to browse the shelves until it was time to go to the farm to see Matthias.

AN HOUR AND A HALF—AND a bag full of new books—later, she pulled up in front of Loretta's house. At least, she hoped it was Loretta's house. There was no sign out front and no house number, but she'd followed the directions Loretta had given her.

The house looked cheery, at least. There were colorful lights strung on the eaves and a wooden sign hanging on the door that read "Welcome." Evvie glimpsed a large barn down a muddy-looking path behind the house, and she heard chickens clucking from somewhere nearby.

She knocked on the door and waited, her hands clasped in front of her.

The door opened, revealing Matthias in a maroon sweater and jeans, his hair a bit rumpled. "Hello," he said. "Come on in." He stepped aside so she could move past him. "I hope you found the house without too much trouble."

She slid her boots off. He held out a hand for her coat, then hung it on a wooden peg on the wall. "I wasn't sure I was in the right place, but I made it," she said.

Evvie stepped into the living room, which was homey. The couch looked well-loved, the coffee table rustic and possibly handmade, and there were plants here and there around the space.

"Can I get you a coffee or tea?" Matthias asked. He hovered at her side, looking unsure of what to do with himself.

"Tea would be lovely, thank you," Evvie said.

The kitchen was attached to the living room, making the whole space open and inviting. Evvie sat at the table as Matthias put the kettle on. The front door opened, letting in a cool breeze. Loretta stepped inside with a chicken under her arm and set it on the floor.

"Hello, Evvie," she said, pushing her hair out of her eyes. "It's nice to see you! Is Matthias getting you tea?"

"Yes, Matthias is getting her tea," Matthias said. "And cookies." He set a plate brimming with sugar cookies shaped like Christmas trees and stars on the table in front of Evvie.

"Ooo, thank you." Evvie looked at him then Loretta in amusement. "And who's this lovely little lady?" she asked, leaning down as the chicken made its way closer to her.

"This is Aphrodite." Loretta beamed at the hen, whose feathers were a gorgeous orange-red color.

"I love her name," Evvie said, then turned her attention to Aphrodite. "Hi there." The chicken paused and looked at her, clucking. "Aren't you a pretty girl?"

Loretta grinned with pride. "All my girls are named after Greek goddesses. Aphrodite is the troublemaker—the chicken, not the goddess."

"Oh, do you cause problems for your mama?" Evvie was well aware she had her pet voice on, but she couldn't help herself. Decades of working in an animal clinic did that to someone. "But I bet she loves you anyway."

"I do," Loretta said, her voice full of affection.

Matthias's deep sigh filled the room. "Etta, really?" Evvie turned to see him standing with a steaming mug, his eyes narrowed at the chicken. "She doesn't have a diaper on. If she shits on the floor, you're cleaning it."

Loretta rolled her eyes. "I was just bringing her in while I got myself a drink. Then we're going back out." She slipped her boots off, which were much muckier than Evvie's, and made her way to the kitchen. Matthias sat across from Evvie as Loretta pulled out an insulated mug and made herself a drink. No one said anything, so Evvie watched Aphrodite explore the room.

"Have fun, you two," Loretta said a minute later, scooping up Aphrodite and sliding her feet into her boots. "I'm sure I'll see you again before you go, Evvie. If I don't come in, come around back to say goodbye!"

"I will." Evvie sipped her tea as Loretta closed the door behind her, leaving the room feeling much emptier. Evvie turned her gaze to Matthias, who was staring at the table. "So," she said, "you're writing a book as well? Or some other project? Loretta didn't give me any details." Evvie wondered if it had something to do with the band, but she didn't want to assume anything.

His shoulders relaxed as if he was relieved she'd started the conversation. "Yeah, yeah. It's . . . well, it's complicated. Sort of. How much writing experience do you have?"

She sat up straighter, feeling like she was in a job interview. "I wrote an entire novel, as you know. It's decades old, which is why I need to revise it before I do anything with it. And it needs some work. I went through a writing phase in my thirties. I joined a writing group and took a few classes. Then I kind of, well, left the story alone until I dug it out of a box a couple weeks ago."

That explanation felt lackluster, but there it was. Saying her experience out loud made her wonder if she was qualified to continue working on her story at all. Who was she to think she could help someone else with their writing? She knew next to nothing about the craft, and publishing was a world she didn't understand yet.

But Matthias nodded, his expression neutral. He didn't seem perturbed at her lack of experience, but he might have been an expert at hiding his thoughts. "That's a lot more experience than I have, that's for sure," he said. "So, how exactly do you think you can help me?"

Evvie opened and closed her mouth, trying not to let those words sting. He had said them nicely, but the wording made it sound like this had been her idea, like she thought she was some kind of expert. "I don't really know," she replied after a couple uncomfortable seconds. "I don't know what you're working on, so I don't know how I can help."

Matthias laughed awkwardly and scratched his jaw, his beard rasping under his nails. "Right, right. I should probably give you details. This project is very . . . private. Etta is the only person here who knows about it, and it's not just my project. There are other people working on it with me. It's important to all of us, and the material is . . . personal."

"Okay . . ." The more he talked around the subject, the more Evvie's curiosity grew. "If you're working on it with others, can't you ask them for help?"

"That's the thing." He rubbed the back of his neck. "They think I started on my part already, but I haven't. And I need to get it done by the first of January."

She nodded slowly, piecing it all together. "And you don't want to tell them you're struggling with it."

He looked at her, his eyes pleading. "Exactly."

Evvie was familiar with feeling nervous about a myriad of things—that seemed to be her default state of being. Pushing through the nervousness was the only way to move forward, and writing a story wasn't any different.

"I want to help, if I can," she said. "So if you tell me what the project is, we can figure out where to go with it."

He nodded and took a deep breath. "Before I tell you, would you be willing to sign an NDA?"

Evvie frowned. An NDA? What was he writing, an exposé on a famous politician? Maybe an insider's look at the music scene?

"I know it's an awkward thing to ask," he continued, "but I'm not comfortable with telling you unless you sign one. I'm sure that makes me sound like a jerk, but I want to cover my bases."

She sipped her tea to give herself time to think. Privacy was important to her too, although she'd never taken it this far. "I wasn't expecting to sign anything, but if it makes you feel comfortable, then sure. Show me where to sign."

CHAPTER TEN

MATTHIAS

*M*atthias went to his room to get his tablet. Etta didn't have a printer, so Evvie would have to sign using his tablet pen. Putting together an NDA was the only real preparation he'd done before Evvie came over. He'd thought about asking Colin to send him a template, but then he'd have to explain why he needed an NDA in the first place. So he'd dug through his emails until he found one he'd had to sign years ago, and he cobbled together his own.

He returned to the kitchen and passed Evvie the tablet. He sat quietly, scratching at a cluster of hives on his forearm, while she read through the document. She seemed satisfied and signed without asking him any questions.

"Alright," she said. "Now tell me why this project is top secret. Are you a spy? Are you under witness protection? Did you kill someone and you're writing a novel about how to hide the evidence?"

He stifled a laugh and cleared his throat. "How do you feel about digging up graves?"

"That depends. Do I have to do the digging, or am I standing guard?" Her mischievous grin was cute, along with the dimple on her cheek.

The laugh he had suppressed bubbled out of him. "Good to know I'll have someone to help me if I ever need to dig up a body. In all seriousness, though, I'm in a band."

"Ah, I see." She didn't look surprised, and his palms began to sweat. But her eyes sparkled, and she leaned forward with her elbows on the table. "Now the NDA makes sense. Iridium Twilight, right?"

"You've heard of us?"

She nodded. "When I first saw you at the bakery, I thought you looked familiar. But I didn't realize who you were until I talked to Dylan, my best friend. She *loves* your band. I've listened to 'Shaken' at least ten times since Saturday."

"Shaken" was the most popular song from their last album.

"Your band is good," Evvie continued. "I suppose I can't tell Dylan about any of this now, though, can I?" She gestured to his tablet.

"Afraid not." Matthias was glad Evvie liked his music and that her friend was a fan, but he was even more glad now that he'd gotten her to sign an NDA.

Evvie frowned slightly then shook it off. "Oh well. You play the drums in the group, right? Do you sing as well?"

He laughed through his nose. "Background vocals only. I'm much better at drumming."

"So are you writing a book about drumming?" The spark in her eyes warmed him, and he was grateful she hadn't asked for an autograph or a selfie. She seemed impressed but not awestruck by his celebrity status, which suited him just fine.

"No. We just came off our farewell tour, and our manager, Colin, wants us to put together a memoir of the band. How the group formed, what our dynamic is like, our ups and downs over the years. Things like that." He explained how each of them was supposed to write their own story, then the ghostwriter would compile it all.

"What a treat!" Evvie wiggled in her seat, and he fought a grin. She was endearing, and he didn't want her to think he was making fun of her. "Dylan will love this—when the book comes out, of course."

He breathed a sigh of relief.

"So what are you struggling with then? It's your story, right? You know it inside and out."

He nodded. "I *should* know it inside and out. But every time I try to write it, or type it, or even speak it, I freeze up."

"Ah, yes." Evvie nodded sagely. "The fear of getting started. I know it well."

"You do?"

"Of course. Every time I work on anything, getting started is the most difficult part. And I imagine that telling your own story —the truth, and nothing but the truth—is even harder."

"That's exactly it," he said, leaning forward. She *got* him. "There's this . . . pressure. What if I say something wrong? What if I don't say enough? What if something I reveal hurts somebody? I appreciate our fans and want to give them our story, but we're people. We have lives like everyone else, and I don't think they need to know every detail of those lives."

Evvie tilted her head slightly, a little *V* forming between her brows as she looked at him. "Do you think telling your story *would* hurt someone? One of your band mates?"

If anyone else had asked him that, he would have thought they were digging for gossip. But Evvie seemed genuinely curious, even concerned.

"Maybe," he said, sighing. "Steven—our bass player—has always been a family man. He's walked the straight and narrow his entire life, and I don't think anything I say would hurt him. But our lead singer, Nick . . . He's gotten into his fair share of trouble. He's not the easiest guy to be friends with, and we've had to dig him out of shit more than once. I think he knows his flaws, but I don't need to air his dirty laundry, do I? He's a good guy, when it comes down to it. But how do I authentically tell the band's story without talking about our struggles as well as our successes?"

He'd been looking at his hands as he spoke, and when he glanced at Evvie, she smiled kindly at him. Like she understood. Like she wasn't judging him for struggling with this. "Sorry," he said. "I don't mean to treat you like a therapist."

"You need to vent, and I'm here for you to vent to," she said. "It's not a problem." She tapped her chin with her pointer finger. "It sounds like—and you can tell me if I'm wrong—you want to get the story perfect. And the pressure you're putting on yourself is keeping you from telling the story at all."

When she put it that way, the problem seemed so clear. How had he not seen it before? "Yeah, yeah. That's it. That's exactly it." Now he knew what was holding him back, but how could he move past it?

Evvie wrapped her hands around her mug and looked at him intently. "I think I know how I can help you now."

"You do?"

She nodded. "You don't have a writing problem. You have a *storytelling* problem. Reframing how you think about your story might help you get started. First, you aren't the one who decides what will go in the book and what will stay out, right?"

"We have veto power before the book gets published. But yeah, I don't get to see all the draft material. Steven might tell something better than I do, or maybe something I say will be completely irrelevant."

"Right. So that's out of your hands. You don't need to worry about it. You said the word *authentic* before, and I think that's key here. Readers—your fans—want a story to connect to. Like you said, you're a person just like they are, so you have similar struggles and joys. They will connect with you because of that. Because of the messiness. As for hurting people, you clearly care for the lead singer . . . ?"

"Nick."

"Right, Nick. You clearly care for Nick even after digging him out of dung-filled situations, and that will show in the way you tell your story. If he doesn't like something you say, he can veto it before the book is published, and you can talk it out with him."

How did she put everything so simply? She made it seem like a walk in the park. But still . . . "If it's that easy, how do I get started?"

She made a popping sound with her lips, and her earrings sparkled as she shook her head. "Oh goodness, I didn't say it would be easy. I wouldn't invalidate you like that. It's going to be hard, but I have an idea."

He threw back the rest of his tea like it was a shot of something stronger, which he could use right about now. "Hit me."

"I don't know about you, but I find it easier to be authentic when I'm talking to a friend. What if you told *me* the story, and we can sort of write it together that way? I know I'm not really your friend"—an implied *yet* made him raise his eyebrows—"but that could work in your favor because you'll phrase things more formally, like you'd probably do when you write." She paused for a moment. "If it's a horrible idea, I understand."

He looked at her, at this earnest and kind woman in front of him, her snowflake earrings and bright blue sweater spot-on for the season. He didn't know much about her at all, and yet the thought of telling her his story seemed like the easiest thing in the world. He could open his mouth now and spill all his secrets to her, and he had the feeling she wouldn't judge him no matter what he said. That she would make him feel heard and understood.

He *wanted* to tell her everything. He wanted to know what she thought. And he didn't know why he wanted that.

"It's not a horrible idea," he said slowly. "I think it's a good one. I'm used to interviews anyway, so it might be useful to have someone there to prompt me with questions. And if you're up for it—for spending an odd amount of time with a man you barely know—then I say, let's do it."

She stuck out her hand. "It's a deal."

He went to shake but then stopped. "Wait," he said. "It's not exactly fair to ask you to help for free. Why don't we work out some kind of payment? Something hourly, or maybe an honorarium?"

She crossed her arms over her chest as if him offering to pay her was an insult. "I don't need money for this. You asked for help, and I said yes. That's all there is to it."

He pressed his lips together. "Okay, but . . . Can't I do *something* in return?" When she went to shake her head, he added, "I'll feel guilty if I don't."

She blew out her lips in a good imitation of a horse and looked up at the ceiling. He stayed quiet, letting her think. A few moments later, she looked at him again. An idea was there, on the tip of her tongue. He could see it, but she seemed reluctant to tell him what it was. He raised an eyebrow.

"Alright," she started. "There is one thing you could help me with. But it's going to sound ridiculous. Like a penguin-riding-a-camel ridiculous."

He snorted. A penguin riding a camel? "After that analogy, I'm not sure it will sound that ridiculous."

She gave him a look that said *You'll see*. "You know I'm writing a novel."

"I do."

"A romance novel, to be specific."

"Yes." He couldn't figure out where she was going with this.

"Well." She twirled her empty mug between her hands, not looking at him. "Everyone says you should write what you know. But I know that's not always true, otherwise we wouldn't have fantasy and science fiction books, right? And there would be psychopath killers everywhere. Anyway, I still think it's valuable to understand your characters and their emotions so you can represent them authentically." She locked eyes with him briefly on the word *authentically* then went back to spinning her mug. "I'm going to tell you something personal now, so brace yourself."

He made a show of preparing himself for whatever she was about to say.

"I've only been on a few dates in the past forty years, and none of them were great. My novel is falling flat because I can't seem to put myself in my protagonist's shoes. I can't grasp that *feeling*, the one people talk about when they're really enjoying their relationship." She was gesturing with her hands now, speaking with them as much as with her words. "Jesus and Judy Garland, this is hard to explain."

She glanced at him, and he nodded for her to keep going.

"I guess what I'm saying is I want to have date-like experiences. I need romantic fodder for my stories. But it doesn't have to be *real* romance, just something to give my story life, to inspire me."

"Like research," he provided.

"Research, yes! I need to go on research trips. And it doesn't feel right to do research for a romance novel alone when romance is all about human interaction and connection."

Now he understood what she was after. "You want me to come on these research trips with you," he said. "Like fake dates."

She blew out a breath. "Yes. In return for me helping you tell your story."

Maybe he should have thought about it more, but the idea of fake dating Evvie didn't seem bad at all. "I'm in," he said, holding out his hand.

"You are?"

"Yeah, 'course." When she went to shake his hand, he pulled back again, just slightly. "You should know, though, that my daughter and granddaughter are staying here for most of December. So if we do this, you'll likely have to spend time with them too. And with Etta."

Evvie smiled, that dimple appearing again. "How old is your granddaughter?"

"She's four." A sense of pride swelled in Matthias's chest as it did every time he spoke about Sophie.

"Oh, perfect. My protagonist has a young child, so I should research family dynamics as well."

The two of them shook on it, and something seemed to travel between their linked hands. Something warm and inviting. Something that made Matthias not want to let go.

CHAPTER ELEVEN

EVVIE

*L*ong after Evvie left the farm, she could feel Matthias's palm against hers. She hadn't expected him to agree to the deal, and she'd been appalled at herself for even suggesting such a thing. Research trips for a romance novel? *Date-like experiences?* She'd been so desperate for a partner for the market that it was all she could come up with.

But he hadn't even really thought about it before saying yes. Was her idea not as strange as she'd thought? Or did he have some other motivation? Regardless, they'd made plans for the market on Wednesday, and she wasn't at all upset about it.

Her mood had made a one-eighty since earlier that day when all her friends had turned her down. Her plans with Matthias might not have been a real date, but he was a looker, and she'd get to spend a few hours with him. They were also going to work on his story on Wednesday, keeping the scales balanced from the start.

All that was missing from her winter plans was snow.

TUESDAY and most of Wednesday flew by so quickly that Evvie barely noticed. She worked on her manuscript, going through and highlighting places that needed more interiority. The story was about a young single mother who moved to a different city for a fresh start. She won a spot on a baking show, and one of her competitors was the love interest. The mother had feelings for the pie maker but struggled with the idea of commitment since her husband had left her and her daughter.

After so many years away from the narrative, it was easy for Evvie to see her writing more objectively. The bones of the story were good, but the gaps in characterization were glaring. When she had written the novel, she'd thought she'd understood her characters. Now, it was clear she hadn't.

But maybe she would after her fake market date.

She drove to Loretta's—Matthias's now, too?—and knocked on the door. Loretta opened it, and Evvie half expected her to be holding a chicken, but she wasn't. She was wearing a white housecoat that had seen better days, the bottom hem fraying and the sleeve cuffs stained.

"Hello," she said, holding the door so Evvie could step inside. "He's just getting ready." She lowered her voice, her eyes twinkling. "I can't remember the last time I saw him put so much effort into his appearance."

Evvie didn't know what to do with that information, and her heartbeat sped slightly. He was dressing up for her? For their fake date? She hoped not, since she had worn a pair of old comfy jeans and a green sweater with a giant polar bear made of sequins on it; she'd wanted to be on theme for the market.

"Sorry to keep you waiting," Matthias said, appearing at the mouth of the hallway. He was in black slacks and a dark red button-up, long-sleeved shirt, the color almost matching the glossy red of his cane. It looked like he was going to a formal concert rather than a market. But Evvie appreciated the effort he'd put in, especially since his shirt fit him perfectly, accentuating his shoulders. He ran a hand over his beard. "Are we ready to go?"

"Yep," Evvie said, rocking back and forth on her feet.

Loretta walked to the couch and collapsed onto it. "Buy me something nice," she said, and Evvie wasn't sure who she was talking to.

"We will," Matthias replied.

The word *we* made Evvie smile. She was part of a *we*! At least, for this evening.

Matthias followed her to her car. "Cute Bug," he said, smiling at her.

"Thank you. Her name is Lady."

"Clever."

Evvie was hyper aware of Matthias as he settled into the seat next to her. He had to push the chair back all the way so his legs could fit, and his head nearly skimmed the roof. She cringed. "Would you rather take your car? You looked a bit . . . squished."

"No, no, I'm fine."

"If you say so." She pulled her phone out of her pocket and opened a transcription app. "Dylan—I think I mentioned her before—is the head librarian at Juniper Creek Library, and I subtly asked her about transcription apps that would help me think out my story ideas. She told me about this free one, so I downloaded it and thought we could give it a go today. See if it's as accurate as it says in the reviews."

He raised his eyebrows and nodded. "That's a good idea. Thank you for doing that."

"I'll start it now so it's ready to go." She pressed the "record" button and handed the phone to him, their palms grazing. Evvie flexed her hand, her skin tingling, as she settled it on the wheel. "You can leave it on your lap or in the cup holder, I think. It should still pick up your voice."

"Sure, sure." He leaned the phone in the cup holder nearest him.

As Evvie started the car, she got a whiff of pine with a tinge of smoke. It reminded her of Christmas trees and bonfires, of drinking hot chocolate out in the snow. Confused, she checked to see if her window was open, but it was firmly shut, and so was Matthias's.

"Is everything okay?" Matthias asked.

"Yes, I just—" She leaned over to look at the back window, which drew her nearer to Matthias. The smell got stronger. It was *him*. Her cheeks flushed. "Ah . . . I thought I had left something in the back, but it's not important."

She cleared her throat and put the car in drive, heading down the dirt road. It was bumpy here, which probably wasn't great for recording, but the road would smooth out as soon as they got on the highway.

"So," she said, keeping her eyes straight ahead, "where would you like to start your story?"

Matthias let out a loud breath, not quite a sigh. "Where do you think I should start?"

"Hmm." She wondered if the recording was making him uncomfortable; she needed to help him forget it was there. "Why did you want to be a musician?"

"Oh, that's an easy question. My dad played the accordion."

"Your dad played the accordion . . . so you started playing the drums? I don't quite see the connection."

"It got me into music," Matthias said. "Dad used to play all kinds of folksy songs on it, especially at family gatherings. Any big dinners, holidays, birthdays . . . he loved music. He showed me how to play, which is how I learned about rhythm. And I think it helped me with my coordination skills too."

She waited for him to continue, but he didn't. He was looking out the passenger-side window, possibly lost in thought.

"When did drums come into the picture?" she prompted gently. She wanted to keep the story going for his sake—this is what she had agreed to help him with, after all—but she was also genuinely interested.

"Hm?" He turned to her. "Oh, when I was a teenager, I think. I reached that age where my parents weren't cool anymore, and I wanted to spend time with my friends more than anyone else. A few of them were into rock music, and one of them had a drum kit. The first time I hit a cymbal . . . man, I was a goner. There's real power in playing the drums, but there's control too.

"When I first started out, I would put so much energy into it and fizzle out quickly, but I learned over the years that drumming is so much more than energy and accuracy. It's also strength, smoothness, and *feeling*. It's the backbone of any song—it keeps the rest of the instruments together. This sounds strange, but there's a melody to drums too. When you really know what you're doing, you can *create* the melody."

His voice was infused with passion, and Evvie couldn't help but smile. She'd felt passionate about many hobbies in her life, but not enough to dedicate so much time and energy to them. Not enough to make a career out of them.

"Did you teach yourself to play?" she asked.

"My friend started teaching me in high school since he took lessons. I was over at his house so much that his parents talked to mine, and eventually, we got some lessons together. I worked in town at the ice cream parlor to save up for my own kit, and when I finally got one, I had to leave it at my friend's house because my parents said the noise wasn't good for the animals. There was no way Mom was going to let me have it in the house, anyway. And Etta would have hated it." He laughed through his nose.

Listening to Matthias talk was better than listening to any podcast. Evvie had never been interested in music before—not in the production side of it, anyway—but his enthusiasm was infectious, and she wanted to know everything he could tell her.

For the next twenty minutes, he told her about the first band he'd joined, how they'd played one gig at a high school dance, but then broke up because of drama over a girl. He was musing about where those guys could be nowadays when they pulled up to Tradex Center in Abbotsford.

"Whoa," he said as they parked. "I can't believe I talked for that entire drive."

Evvie picked up her phone and stopped the recording. "You

did," she said, grinning. She showed him the transcript on the app, scrolling through the words. "Look how much you wrote."

He scoffed. "I didn't *write* that. I said all of that."

"But now it's in writing," she said, waving the phone. "Your story has begun."

He smiled at her, and there was a moment when Evvie thought he might lean over and hug her, but he opened the car door instead.

"The market's in here?" he asked, staring at the tall blue building before them.

The word TRADEX loomed over them in large red letters, and windows took up most of the building's height. Lights twinkled inside, and instrumental Christmas music filtered out the doors as a few customers left. Evvie had been to a pet lover's show and a vintage market at the event center before, but every time she'd tried to go to the Christmas market, something got in the way.

Not this year. This year she was here to enjoy herself, and she wasn't alone.

"Yep, it's in here," Evvie said. She grabbed a few cloth bags out the backseat of the Bug; there was no way she'd be leaving the market empty-handed. Plus, Matthias had promised to get something for Loretta. She took off her coat and threw it in the car so she wouldn't have to carry it around, revealing her polar bear sweater.

Matthias looked down at the black jacket he'd thrown over his button-up and raised an eyebrow. "I feel underdressed."

"I'm sure we can find you an ugly sweater if you want to fit in," Evvie said, grinning.

"Do you think they have a Hanukkah one?"

Evvie tilted her head. "Why Hanukkah?"

"I'm Jewish," Matthias replied with a half shrug.

"Oh! Goodness, I'm sorry, I didn't know. So you don't celebrate Christmas?" She thought of the Christmas lights on the farmhouse, confused.

He waved a hand. "I celebrate both, and I'm not super religious. My parents were more observant, but Etta and I sort of lost touch with Judaism when we moved out. I'd like Beatrice and Sophie to know more of their heritage, though."

"That makes sense." There was a synagogue in Abbotsford, but Evvie didn't know any Jewish people personally. The Fraser Valley, as far as she could tell, was largely Catholic, Christian, and Muslim. She paused, not knowing what else to say. "Shall we go in?"

"Let's. So what's the plan here?" Matthias asked as they went inside.

They each paid their own entrance fee, and Evvie stopped at the side of the center aisle, joy bubbling up inside her at all the holiday cheer surrounding them. Giant sparkly snowflakes hung from the ceiling, and the scent of cinnamon and cloves permeated the air. "What do you mean, *the plan*? We're here to enjoy ourselves. To walk around, to eat food, and to feel positively Christmasy. And Hanukkah-y?"

He grinned. "That's a good plan if I've ever heard one." Matthias held out his arm, so she linked hers through his, and they meandered up the aisle. Evvie let him set the pace, aware of his cane.

It was the first night the market was open, but it wasn't too busy. The weekend would be much busier, which is why Evvie wanted to go on a weeknight. Later, many of the vendors would be sold out of the best goods.

"Let's find a drink first," she said. "That way we can sip and scan."

"Sip and scan?" Matthias had to look down at her as he spoke because of their height difference, and the lack of space between them was pleasantly intimate.

"Sip the drink and scan the wares. It's the best way to experience any market. By the time you've seen everything, your drink is done, so you can get rid of the cup and free up your hands for all the goodies!"

Matthias laughed, and she felt it rumble through his body. "One hand, in my case," he said. "Although I can probably hang a bag or two off my cane."

They found a stall selling hot cocoa made from gourmet chocolate bombs. Evvie ordered one full of edible glitter, and Matthias asked for a hazelnut hot chocolate. While they waited, Matthias smiled at her, a small satisfied-looking smile without showing his teeth. He didn't say anything, he just kept smiling. Blood rushed to Evvie's cheeks.

"What is it?" she asked. "Do I have something on my face? I haven't even had the hot chocolate yet, so unless glitter has gotten even better at covering every gosh darn thing in sight, I can't have any of that on my face." She wiped her cheeks anyway to be safe.

Matthias shook his head, that smile still gracing his lips. Even though Evvie didn't understand his expression, she liked that she was the one to put it there.

CHAPTER TWELVE

MATTHIAS

*I*n his seventy-four years, Matthias hadn't met anyone as thoughtful and kind as Evvie. He'd only known her for a few days, and yet he felt safe around her, like he could be himself and not hold back. She didn't pry into his life like so many other people had done, especially people he'd dated.

This wasn't really a date, though. It was a fake date.

As the barista handed them their hot chocolates, he said, "I appreciate you not prodding me for information, even though you're helping me tell my story."

"That's a specific circumstance," Evvie replied.

"Even so."

They started walking up the aisle, past stalls selling organic peanut butter, handmade earrings, eccentric pottery, and wooden signs.

Evvie went up to a business selling all different kinds of fudge. "We have to come back to this one for sure," she said.

He sipped his hot chocolate, surprised at how good it was. The vendors weren't lying when they said *gourmet*. "Let's go back to that fancy drink stall later, too. I want to get a hot chocolate bomb for Etta," he said, thinking of how the "bomb"—a ball of milk chocolate—had transformed into the decadent drink in his hand when the vendor had poured hot milk over it. Etta would love it.

"Good idea." Evvie walked up to a table selling candles, and he caught a glimpse of her earrings. They had little dangling red-and-green plaid bows. "Smell this." She held out a candle to him.

It smelled like a forest on a crisp winter day—kind of like his cologne, actually.

"I'm going to get this one when we come back around." She turned to the vendor, a burly man with braids in his beard. "Can you put this aside for me, please?"

He took it from her cheerfully and placed it beneath the table.

They continued walking, and Matthias enjoyed every minute of it more than he thought possible. Evvie's eyes lit up at so many things, and she ended up talking to more than one vendor about their business. They came across a kiosk full of menorahs, dreidels, and Hanukkah-themed decor, and Matthias happily explained what he could about the holiday. "I'd like to get a dreidel for my granddaughter." He'd already stocked up on gelt for her.

"And this sweater," Evvie said, holding up a blue sweater that said "This is how I roll" beside an image of a dreidel.

Matthias shook his head, raising his eyebrows. "I dunno about that one."

"I'll get it for you then."

He tried to wrestle it away from her, but she managed to fend him off, giggling as she handed her card to the vendor. "You said you wanted an ugly sweater anyway," she said, pushing the bag at him. "Happy Hanukkah."

He couldn't even pretend to be upset at her. This was his first Hanukkah sweater, and he knew Etta, Bea, and Sophie would love it. Before they left the stall, he bought them all sweaters to match it.

By the time he and Evvie had walked up and down all the aisles, Evvie had collected more business cards than he could remember.

"Oh my stars, look at this!" He followed her to a booth that stood out from the others. Black velvet lined the walls, tables, and even the ceiling that had been put on the stall. The table inside displayed earthy-looking structures—logs, mushrooms, dried flowers, stones—all containing a glowing gemstone. "I have to get one of these for Eleanor," Evvie breathed. She handed him her empty cup of hot chocolate, and her hands fluttered over the wares. "These are beautiful," she told the vendor, a woman with long pink hair and black cat-eye glasses.

He could tell this choice would take a while, so he went to throw their now-empty cups in the garbage can by the wall outside the booth. By the time he got back to the table, Evvie was asking the vendor about the meaning of each gemstone.

"Which one do you think would be better?" Evvie asked him, gesturing at two different glowing art pieces that reminded him of fairy homes. "This yellow one brings good health, and the purple one is for luck."

He stroked his beard as he looked at them. "Eleanor is a florist, right? Why don't you get her the one for luck? She could put it in her shop for good business."

"Oh, great idea, Matthias."

The sound of his name in her mouth gave him goosebumps—the kind that made you shiver with pleasure. He wanted to ask her to say his name again, but that would be more than creepy. At least, in this scenario. He had to keep reminding himself that this date was *fake*.

With her gift in hand, Evvie practically skipped over to him. "Can we look at the Christmas trees before we go back for our goodies?" One aisle they'd wandered earlier was lined with decorated trees, all the colored lights and ornaments creating an extra festive atmosphere. "The one that gets the most votes wins a prize for charity!"

"Of course. We'll have to vote carefully, then."

They took their time looking at the trees, pretending they

were experts in the art of tree decoration. At one point, Matthias said, "I haven't had a Christmas tree for years."

Evvie gasped. "You haven't?"

"No, we usually spend Christmas at Nick's house. I never saw the point in decorating my own."

Evvie shot him a stern look. "We'll have to fix that this year. You can't spend Christmas without a Christmas tree, especially since you'll be with your family. Does Loretta get a tree?"

He frowned. "I dunno. I haven't asked."

"I can help you pick one out. There's a fantastic Christmas tree farm between here and Juniper Creek, and you can roast marshmallows and make s'mores there. They even deliver the tree for you! It's wonderful."

He wasn't sure how this fit into their deal, but he wasn't about to say no to spending more time with Evvie. "I'll hold you to that," he said.

An hour later, Evvie's bags were full, Matthias had three bags of his own, and they were ready to head home.

He was too tired to continue with his story on the ride back, so Evvie put on the radio, and the two of them were quiet, the mood comfortable. Evvie's lips were turned up slightly, as if even driving brought her joy. Was there anything that made this woman *unhappy*? If there was, he didn't want to see it.

She glanced at him and caught him looking at her. "Do I actually have glitter on my face this time?"

"No," he said. "You just seem happy. Was that the type of date-like experience you were looking for?"

The dimple on her cheek appeared again. "Yes, I believe so. I understand my heroine a bit better now."

"Good. Do you have another research trip in mind? Besides going Christmas tree hunting?"

"Hmm. There's a paint night at Cedar Logs art gallery if you're interested in that, or we could go on a holiday light walk to see the glorious lights people put up this year."

"We could do both, if we have time."

"You would do both?"

With his mood high after going to the market with her, he would do just about anything to see her smile. "I would."

"Okay. Well, I'll see when the next paint night is, and we can make a plan . . . for our next research trip."

"Our next *date*"—he paused and she glanced at him—"like experience."

She smirked. "Yes, that."

AFTER EVVIE LEFT, Matthias's mood didn't drop, but his energy did after he'd been sitting on the couch for five minutes. His feet were sore, which he hadn't noticed before, but he had no regrets.

"Tired?" Etta asked from her spot on the chair. She'd been sketching when he got home.

He grunted in response, his eyelids heavy as he leaned his head back on the couch cushion.

"Why don't you go to bed?"

He yawned. "I will, in a bit." Closing his eyes, he listened to her pencil scratch softly across the paper.

"So how was the market?"

"Good."

"Did you get me something?"

"Mm-hmm. But you don't get to have it yet."

"Fine." She paused. "How exactly does a market trip help with your memoir, again?" Matthias hadn't told Etta the details of his deal with Evvie, only that the two of them had worked out something to benefit them both.

He waved a hand. "Tell you later."

Just as he was drifting to sleep, his cell phone rang. He sat up with a start and blinked a few times, trying to wake himself up. Bea's name blinked on his phone screen.

"Hey, Dad," she said when he picked up. "Just checking in to finalize our plans."

They confirmed the dates Bea and Sophie would visit, then Bea insisted on letting him go because he kept yawning. "Okay," Matthias said. "Well, we're both excited to have you over, baby. You and Sophie both."

"We're excited too, right, Soph?"

In the background, Matthias heard Sophie yell, "Yeah!" in her high-pitched four-year-old voice. He chuckled.

"Perfect. See you then."

One week until his daughter and granddaughter came to stay. He hadn't had this much time with family in years. He didn't know if he even remembered how to function for a prolonged period of time around kids. What if he swore in front of her? A bolt of panic hit him—he hadn't gotten any gifts besides the sweaters and the dreidel! What did four-year-olds like? What would Bea like?

And the house! It was clean enough, but it wasn't ready for Hanukkah or Christmas. The only decorations they had up were the lights outside on the eaves. He wanted everything to be perfect when Bea and Sophie got there. He'd been absent for most of Bea's life, and he had a lot to make up for.

A Christmas tree. That's where he could start. "Etta, do you have a Christmas tree?"

"Just a small one. Why?"

Matthias remembered Evvie's gasp at the market. She'd be horrified at Etta's tiny tree. "Do you mind if we get a real tree this year?"

Etta perked up. "I'd love that."

"Perfect." He pulled out his phone and texted Evvie:

> Tree shopping soon? Guests coming next week . . .

She answered less than a minute later.

The weekend will be busy. Monday?

Yes . . . thanks . . .

At least that would be taken care of now, and the thought of seeing Evvie again made him straighten. He heaved himself off the couch with the help of his cane, the pain in his knee making him wince, and went to get the hot chocolate bombs from his bag.

"How do you feel about a late dessert?" he asked Etta.

He hoped the sugar boost would give him the energy he needed to go through the transcript Evvie had sent him from the app. He'd need to download the app himself later so he could continue his story. After starting it in Evvie's car, it didn't seem as scary anymore.

CHAPTER THIRTEEN

EVVIE

*A*s soon as Evvie got home from the market, she pulled out a notebook and jotted down everything she could remember from the outing: the different vendors, the Christmas trees, snippets of conversations she'd overheard. And how she'd felt being there with Matthias.

Although these research trips were meant to help her understand her characters' feelings better, she thought they'd also help her come up with a few action beats or notes about human interaction in general. Instead, she'd come home with a good idea of how people felt on a real date.

At least, she *thought* that's how people felt.

The energy, the comfort, the longing . . . for a smile, a touch, a nod, a thought. Being with Matthias had been effortless. She'd been nervous, of course, but in a way that excited her rather than made her want to throw up.

It made her reconsider whether dating was for her. But Matthias wasn't looking for anyone either; he only needed help with his memoir.

She was still floating on a cloud as she made herself a cup of tea. Ideally, she'd call Dylan and tell her all about her day, but Dylan was with Frankie and her family in Vancouver.

The thought of Dylan jolted her. Dylan loved Iridium Twilight, which meant she'd pry about the project they were working on. Not only was Dylan a fan, but Matthias had been a couple grades ahead of Dylan in school. Minnie and Frankie didn't care about Matthias and his band the way Dylan did, but they knew who he was too; even if they didn't move in the same circles back then, they'd all grown up in Juniper Creek. Evvie would have to watch what she said around them so she didn't break the NDA. She was sure they wouldn't gossip about it, but a deal was a deal.

She curled up on the couch with her tea, determined to respect Matthias's privacy and still basking in the afterglow of the market.

Had she felt this way with Simon, her ex-husband? They'd started dating in high school and stayed together for years. She'd been young and vibrant then, full of potential, her whole life stretching ahead of her. Everything had seemed shiny and adventurous, including Simon. And they had been happy together, once.

She'd never been able to pinpoint when their relationship turned, or what she had done to make it go downhill.

When she went to sip her tea again, it was cold. How long had she been sitting there, thinking about one of the worst days of her life? She'd been riding a high, and now she felt so low.

She popped her tea in the microwave, and her phone pinged. Matthias's name made her mood shift again, and a few minutes later they had plans to get a Christmas tree together.

When she settled into bed with a romance novel, she let herself soak in the joy she'd felt that day.

THE NEXT DAY, she buckled down and revised as much of her manuscript as she could before going to the queer seniors' night. Delicious tension swirled between her heroine and the love interest as they danced around the idea of being in a relationship. Evvie's confidence grew as she added details to show how the heroine felt every time the pie maker smiled or brushed her hand.

She was still thinking about her story on the drive to Abbotsford, but then her thoughts shifted to Matthias. She debated what she'd tell her friends about him. Going to the market had been her highlight of the week, without a doubt, but she didn't want to explain the deal she and Matthias had made—it was an odd deal to begin with, and Evvie couldn't reveal anything about what Matthias was working on. She wasn't even sure if she could use his name safely with this friend group. Were any of them Iridium Twilight fans?

And if she told them she'd gone to the market with a man, they'd assume it was a date, even if she said it wasn't. It had felt like a date, but it wasn't one.

Not to mention how they'd all reacted about dates with men the week before. Was Evvie becoming less queer somehow because of her fake date with Matthias? And how would her friends react when they found out her romance novel was about a woman falling in love with a man?

All these thoughts kept her butt rooted to the driver's seat in the community center parking lot until she was fifteen minutes late. If she kept sitting there, she might as well not go in. Shaking her head at herself, she got out of the car and hurried inside.

There was a chorus of "Evvie!" as she walked in. She waved to everyone and poured herself a cup of tea at the table, forgoing the brownies someone had brought because anxiety filled her stomach.

"You missed the highs and lows," Gem said as Evvie sat down. "But we haven't started tonight's activity, so go ahead and share yours."

She blew on her tea to give herself a moment. "Well, my low was that Dylan and Frankie went away for the week, and they won't be back until Sunday night. I'm glad they get time with family, but I miss Dylan."

"Aw." Noah patted her arm.

"Sorry, who is Dylan?" Tom asked.

"My best friend," Evvie said. He nodded, and she continued, "And my high was going to a Christmas market. I got gifts for all my friends, so I'm all set for the holidays."

There. That wasn't a lie, and it didn't bring dating or men anywhere near the conversation.

"Oh, was it the market you mentioned in the Facebook group?" Priya asked.

Evvie gave everyone details about the market, then they played Ticket to Ride for the rest of the evening. Priya won, as usual, but Tom got the longest route. Evvie came in last, which she expected since her mind wasn't on the game.

She wondered what Matthias was doing that evening. Did he and Loretta play games together? If he liked Ticket to Ride, she could bring it over to play with his family. Although, his granddaughter was four, which was probably too young to play. Maybe there was a different game that would work for everyone.

But what was she thinking, assuming she would be playing games with Matthias's family? They had an agreement to help each other with their projects, and that was it. They were friendly, but not truly friends—not yet—and their partnership would likely be finished before Christmas. For sure before January, when Matthias's story was due.

Who gave a flap if Dylan was with Frankie and her family? Evvie was going to phone her that evening when she got home. She needed someone to help her work out her feelings, someone she could trust more than anyone else. She needed her best friend.

CHAPTER FOURTEEN

MATTHIAS

*T*he weekend crawled by, probably because Matthias wished it was Monday. He couldn't sit around waiting, so he tried to talk out more of his story. Evvie had texted him the name of the app, so now he could record himself speaking whenever he wanted.

He sat in his room and tried to continue where he'd left off, but he felt ridiculous and self-conscious speaking to an empty room. Then he'd tried telling his story to Etta, but she already knew much of it, so he kept editing out pieces that should probably be there, and Etta kept filling in the gaps. It made the story choppy.

He stopped his latest recording and laid his head on the kitchen table. "This isn't working," he said. *I need to talk to Evvie.*

Etta sucked her teeth. "I know how you can clear your mind."

"You do?" he said, lifting his head to look at her.

She nodded. "Help me clean the coop."

He groaned. "Really, Etta?"

"Really. It's physical movement, and you'll get fresh air. I haven't done a deep clean in a while because it's difficult to do on my own. Aren't you here to help me, anyway?"

Of course, she'd pulled the guilt card. He glared at her. "Fine, let's go."

Cleaning the coop wasn't as bad as he'd expected. He leaned on his cane and held a garbage bag open for Etta while she scooped straw and dirt and chicken shit into it. Standing out there with the chickens clucking reminded him of being a kid, helping his parents around the farm. He didn't often miss milking cows and shoveling manure, but in that moment, he did.

"So there's Persephone, Circe, Aphrodite . . . ?"

"Artemis and Athena," Etta said.

"Right, gotcha."

Etta babbled on about her chickens, and he did his best to listen as they worked. When they were done, they sat on a bench outside the chicken wire and watched the hens move in and out of their newly cleaned home.

Tapping her messy rubber boots together, Etta said, "Is this Christmas tree thing with Evvie tomorrow a date?"

"What? No. It's not a date." He brushed a piece of straw off his jeans.

"Can I come with you then?"

He caught himself before he blurted *No!* Why couldn't she go with them? It really wasn't a date, and the fact that Etta wanted to go out and do something was a good sign; she only wanted to leave the farm when she was feeling well. He needed to take advantage of it.

"I'm sure Evvie won't have a problem with that," he said. "Let me double check with her, but I think it will be fun to have you there. When's the last time you went to get a Christmas tree?"

She leaned her head against the wall of the house. "I've never gone. I had no reason to when I lived with Mom, and I bought that small fake tree after she passed. I didn't need a big tree for myself."

Matthias cringed at the implication that Etta had been spending Christmas alone. And it was his fault. He should have come up to visit her, but he'd been selfish.

This year, he wouldn't be. "This Christmas, we're going to have the best tree." He hit the ground with his cane for emphasis.

"What if we find a cute Charlie Brown tree instead?" Etta said, elbowing him lightly.

"Who says a Charlie Brown tree can't be the best tree?"

"Touché."

They stayed outside for a few more minutes until Etta said her feet were going numb, and Matthias found himself looking forward to having his sister with them the next day.

As Matthias had suspected, Evvie hadn't had a problem with Etta tagging along. When they met at the tree lot, she gave Etta a warm smile. "It's your tree too, so you *should* be here."

Evvie wore her puffy winter coat with her rainbow knitted scarf and a matching toque. She was a walking rainbow much of the time; Matthias hadn't seen her wear any dark or neutral colors yet. She smiled brightly at him, and he wanted to link arms with her again like they had at the market, but Etta was there. The whole dynamic was different with his sister around.

"So, how do we do this?" Etta asked, zipping her coat up to her chin.

It wasn't raining today, thankfully, but the air had a crispness to it, and the chill worked its way under his layers.

"We walk around, find the tree we want, tell the owners, and they'll organize delivery for us. For you, I mean. Since it's your tree." Evvie's cheeks were tinged pink, but Matthias couldn't tell if it was from what she'd said or from the cold. "But first, we get hot chocolate."

"I doubt theirs will beat the hot chocolate bombs," Matthias said as they followed Evvie to a kiosk.

"Those were amazing," Etta agreed.

Once they got their orders, they wandered through the maze of trees. It was impossible for Matthias to look for a Christmas tree without thinking of the market. "There are no decorations to judge on these ones," he said.

"Nope," Evvie replied, popping the *p*. "You have to use your imagination. What kind of tree do you like, Loretta?" She was better at keeping his sister in their conversation than he was.

"I'm not sure." Etta scrutinized the trees they passed. "We don't want anything too tall because it would hit the ceiling. But it has to be big enough to fill the living room without crowding it."

Earlier that morning, he and Etta had shifted furniture around, making space in front of the living room window for the tree. It would block the natural light, but they'd be able to see it twinkling in the window whenever they came home, and it didn't make sense to put it anywhere else.

"What about this one?" Evvie gestured at a slightly lopsided tree. "It has character."

Etta held her hot chocolate between her mittened palms. "Hmm. Maybe. Can we keep looking?"

"You don't like it?" Matthias asked. "I think it would work nicely."

Etta smirked. "You're just saying that because Evvie likes it."

"What? No, I'm not."

At this point, Evvie strode on as if she couldn't hear them, although he was sure she'd been listening.

"Etta," he hissed at his sister. "Can you please refrain from making things awkward?"

His sister snorted. "How am I making things awkward? It's clear that you like her. She'd be witless not to see it."

Matthias gritted his teeth. "She's helping me with the memoir, and I'm helping her with her novel, okay? That's it. There's nothing else going on."

"Right. Sure. Whatever you say." With a wave, she followed Evvie.

The three of them walked around for another twenty minutes

or so, the bottom of Matthias's cane caked with mud by the time they finally decided to go with the tree Evvie had pointed out.

"You know what," Etta said, "you're right. It does have character." She smirked again at Matthias, and he glared at her.

Once their delivery details were worked out, the three of them went over to a firepit surrounded by benches. There had been a few people there earlier, but now it was vacant, although the fire was still going. A worker approached as they held their hands over the flames. "Would you like to roast a marshmallow?" they asked.

"Oh, yes, please!" Evvie said, taking a roasting stick and sliding a marshmallow on it.

Etta asked Matthias to make hers, so he slid two marshmallows on his roasting stick. "These flames are a bit big for roasting marshmallows, aren't they?" he asked.

"You just have to be more careful," Evvie said, holding her marshmallow a good distance from the fire. "And patient."

Matthias tried to follow her example but ended up burning both marshmallows, as usual. He'd never been able to make the perfectly golden treat that Evvie's was turning into. Etta didn't seem to mind, declining the graham crackers and chocolate and shoving the whole marshmallow in her mouth. She smiled at him with sealed lips, her cheeks slightly puffed out.

He shook his head at her and laughed, doing the same thing.

"I'm running to the washroom," Etta said, heading toward the small gift shop at the edge of the parking lot.

When she left, Matthias shifted closer to Evvie.

"There we go." Evvie pulled her marshmallow away from the fire. "Can you prep a s'more for me?"

He grabbed two graham crackers and a square of chocolate then used them to slide the marshmallow off Evvie's roasting stick as she held it steady.

"Thank you!" She beamed at him as she took her first bite, marshmallow oozing out the sides of the s'more, some of it sticking to her chin. She didn't seem bothered by the mess, finishing up her s'more and thanking the worker when they handed her a wet wipe.

"This reminds me of summer camp," Evvie said, looking wistfully at the fire as she slid her gloves back on. "Except those nights were much warmer." She shifted closer to him until their arms touched.

"Evvie? Fancy seeing you here!" Evvie shifted away again as two women came up to them. The woman who spoke was Black, her blue winter coat so long that it covered her knees. She wore a rainbow scarf just like Evvie's. The white woman next to her was visibly shivering, her shoulders up around her ears. She got as close to the fire as she could without stepping right into it.

"Gem?" Evvie said. "Hello! How are you?"

"Good, we're picking out our tree. I'm going to spend Christmas with Margie's family this year, so we're getting everything ready for the kids."

"It's going to be a full house," the other woman—Margie, she must be—said over her shoulder. "The first time Gem will be with all of us at once. I told her to prepare herself."

Evvie laughed along with Gem, her hand over her mouth. "I'm sure I'll be fine," Gem said, shooting a fond but exasperated look at Margie. "And who's this?" She turned her gaze to Matthias.

Evvie froze for a second, and Matthias wasn't sure if she would answer. Right when he was about to introduce himself, she finally spoke.

CHAPTER FIFTEEN

EVVIE

It was like her brain had stopped working. She understood that Gem had asked who Matthias was, but she seemed unable to make her mouth move to answer the question.

Finally, she managed to say, "Um, this is Matthias." She cleared her throat. "Matthias, this is Gem and Margie." Cheese and rice, her heart was beating a mile a minute. Why was she panicking?

"Nice to meet you, Matthias," Gem said, shaking Matthias's hand. At the same time, she widened her eyes at Evvie as if to say *Why didn't you tell us about this guy?*

Evvie shrugged.

"So how do you two know each other?" Margie asked. The fire seemed to have warmed her up—she was no longer shivering. Now, she was looking back and forth between Matthias and Evvie, her eyebrows raised expectantly.

"We, um . . ." Why was Evvie's brain malfunctioning? They were friends! Why was that so difficult to say?

"I'm back," Loretta said, striding into the circle. "Oh, hello. Am I interrupting?"

"No," Evvie said. "This is Gem and Margie, friends of mine.

This is Loretta, Matthias's sister. We just picked out a tree. They live on a farm, it's extraordinarily cute. You'd like it, I think. Very homey. Lots of plants. The tree will fit right in. And they have family coming too, so it will also be a full house! Lots of cheer, so many fun Christmas things. And Hanukkah, since they're Jewish." First, she couldn't get herself to speak, and now she couldn't get herself to shut up. Whatever was happening, she wanted out. She glanced at Matthias. "We should get going, though, right?"

Without waiting for him to answer, she grabbed his hand and pulled him toward the parking lot. "I'll see you two on Thursday!" she called to Gem and Margie. "Enjoy the s'mores!"

She trusted that Loretta was walking after them as she kept going, trying not to pull Matthias too quickly because of his knee.

"Are you alright?" he asked, laughing breathlessly as she finally stopped at the edge of the parking lot. "What was that about?"

Fudge nuggets. How was she going to explain that mess? "My friends can be . . . Well, I just . . . I wasn't expecting to see them here, is all. With you. And Loretta."

"In a hurry, are we?" Loretta asked as she caught up to them.

"Yes, I need to get home and work on my manuscript. Sorry, that was rather abrupt of me." Evvie forced a laugh, the fakeness of it grating on her ears. "But this was fun! We should do it again sometime." The more she talked, the more she wanted to put her foot in her mouth. "Text me later to organize memoir work?" she said to Matthias.

She stood up on her tiptoes, leaning toward him, and he seemed to know what she was after, lowering his head. She pressed a light kiss to his cheek, waved at Loretta, and hurried to her Bug.

It wasn't until she sat down and had her seatbelt on that she realized what she'd just done. She'd kissed Matthias. In front of Loretta! It was on the cheek, but still. Why had she done that? It had felt like the thing to do, like she did it all the time. Like kissing Matthias was normal.

She was so mortified, she didn't remember the drive home.

One second, she was in the parking lot, and the next, she was making tea at her counter.

"This is fine," she muttered under her breath. "Everything is fine."

But she felt like a mess. She did the one thing she knew would help her feel better: she called Dylan.

"I'll be right over," Dylan said after she explained the situation.

When Dylan got there, Evvie had bowls of baking ingredients strewn across the counter and a double batch of cookies in the mixer.

"Stress baking?" Dylan asked, pushing a hand through her wet hair. It must have been raining. Evvie sighed, longing once again for snow.

"Maybe." Evvie turned off the mixer. She grabbed three cookie sheets and lined them with baking mats. As she scooped out balls of cookie dough, Dylan washed her hands, then joined Evvie and started rolling the dough in a bowl of sugar. "Thanks," Evvie said, lightly bumping Dylan's hip with her own.

"Ginger molasses?"

"Yep."

"My favorite."

"I know."

"So you kissed Matthias on the cheek, hey?" Dylan's voice bubbled with excitement. "Is that what's got you in a tizzy?"

Evvie used her shoulder to push a strand of hair out of her face. "I don't think so. The kiss was unexpected, but it was just on the cheek. Matthias didn't seem to mind, anyway. I think I'm more shocked at my own behavior with Gem and Margie. Why did I react that way?"

"Shit," Dylan said as she dropped a piece of dough. She picked it up and popped it in her mouth. "Five-second rule."

Evvie laughed through her nose and kept scooping.

"It sounds to me like you were nervous to be seen out with Matthias and Loretta. But mostly Matthias. Am I right?"

"Yes, but why? Why was I nervous? It's not like I was doing anything wrong."

"Of course not. And you're not usually one to be nervous around your friends." Dylan popped another piece of dough in her mouth, and Evvie lightly slapped her hand.

"You won't get any baked ones if you keep eating the dough," Evvie scolded.

Dylan shrugged, and Evvie's text notification went off. She washed her hands, hoping it was Matthias. Evvie's heart sank when she saw Gem's name on the screen. Biting her lip, she opened the message.

> It was nice to see you today. Are you and
> Matthias dating? You should bring him to our
> meeting tomorrow!

Evvie groaned and Dylan raised an eyebrow at her, so she showed her friend the text.

"Ah," Dylan said, nodding. "*That's* why you were so nervous."

"What do you mean?"

"That text message." Dylan gestured to Evvie's phone with her chin, and a wave of anxiety flowed through Evvie's chest. "You knew what Margie and Gem would think, seeing you with Matthias. They'd think you were dating, and you didn't want that."

Evvie thought over her friend's words for a moment, and they made sense. "How do you know the inner working of my brain better than I do?" She scowled.

"What can I say? It's a librarian thing."

"I think it's a Dylan thing. In any case, you're right." How had she not seen it before? "Now I have to tell them I'm *not* dating Matthias." The thought of it made her chest unexpectedly tight.

Dylan's voice softened. "And you don't want to tell them

because you wish you *were* dating him. And I may be a lesbian, but I don't blame you."

Evvie froze for a second then nodded, tears filling her eyes. She squeezed her lids shut, setting a few drops free. "I don't want to like him like that."

"Why is liking him a bad thing?" Dylan asked, her voice still gentle. "You wanted to spend this Christmas with someone, right? I know you don't like being the odd one out."

"What? No, I'm fine, I—"

Dylan held up a hand. "Ev, it's okay that it bothers you. And I know you're happy for me and Frankie, and for Minnie and Eleanor, but I also know I haven't been able to spend as much time with you. And you're retired. And you're watching everyone fall in love around you. I *know* you."

Evvie wiped her tears with her sweater sleeve.

"You deserve someone who will make you happy, if that's what you want. You're a fucking diamond. Anyone would be lucky to be with you."

Evvie sniffled. "Can I hug you?"

"If you have to," Dylan said, pressing her lips together in a smile.

Evvie wrapped her arms around Dylan and squeezed her.

She didn't feel like a diamond. Most of the time, she replayed the embarrassing things she'd done in the past and felt like that was all people could see. She threw herself into helping people to make them like her more, to make sure she wasn't a burden in any way.

The thought that anyone would be lucky to have her . . . She wanted to believe Dylan so badly. She wanted to believe she could have a chance with Matthias, that he'd maybe say yes if she asked him on a real date. But she didn't want to risk the friendship they'd started.

"He's going to text me tonight," she said. "We need to organize another time to work on his story."

"Are you going to bring up your feelings for him then?" Dylan asked.

"I don't know. I don't know if I'm ready for that."

"There's no rush, Ev. You're not on a deadline."

"I know. Thank you."

Dylan helped her finish the cookies, clearly trying her best not to dig for details about Matthias, and she took home a container for herself and Frankie. Evvie put another container aside for Minnie and Eleanor; she could drop it off at one of their shops the next morning. She needed to talk to Minnie about the proposal anyway.

She made herself dinner with her phone on the table beside her. Then she worked on her romance novel, feeling more connected to her heroine than ever.

Both nervous. Both pining. Both wrestling with feelings they didn't want.

CHAPTER SIXTEEN

MATTHIAS

*M*atthias had been looking forward to texting Evvie, but he didn't want to do it right when they got home; she'd seemed busy when she left the Christmas tree lot.

On the drive back to the farm, Etta had bugged him about the kiss. He hadn't been bothered at all, though. He'd put on a good act, telling Etta it was nothing, but he was surprised he wasn't glowing.

It was just a kiss on the cheek, and maybe that didn't mean much for Evvie, but it meant a lot to him. He thought there'd been something between them at the market, and now he was sure of it. This hadn't been what he'd intended when he'd asked for her help, but if their relationship moved past friendship, he wouldn't complain.

As long as he managed to see her and his family at the same time. Bea and Sophie were coming on Wednesday, so he and Etta needed to pull out the holiday decorations. Their tree would be delivered the next morning, so at least that was handled.

Everything was going almost *too* well, and part of him waited for the other shoe to drop. Nothing would go wrong, though, because he'd already decided this would be the best December ever.

He promised himself he'd text Evvie after dinner, and it took a ridiculous amount of willpower to eat the pasta Etta made at a normal pace instead of wolfing it down.

Her voice cut through his thoughts. "Matthias, did you hear me?" He blinked at his sister a few times, and she frowned. "I said we should leave the tree to decorate when Bea and Sophie get here."

"Oh. Yes, yes we should. Good idea."

He tried to pay attention to the rest of the dinner conversation, guilty that his mind was elsewhere. He'd come to Juniper Creek for Etta, and now he was struggling to focus on her. When she said she was going to bed early—looking for a tree had tired her out—a shameful jolt of excitement went through his chest.

Once she'd gone to bed, he was free to text Evvie without ignoring Etta. He changed into his plaid pajama pants and laid back on the couch with *Far and Wide*, one of the travel memoirs by Neil Peart, the drummer from Rush. He'd been one of Matthias's favorite drummers, and they'd even gone out for a meal a few times together. Neil's passing in 2020 had crushed Matthias.

Before he opened the book, he shot Evvie a text asking how she was doing. He hadn't even opened the front cover before she replied, as if she'd been waiting beside her phone.

Good. Working on my novel. You?

Reading . . .

He wanted to phone her, to hear her voice, but she'd specifically asked him to *text* her.

Still good to help me . . . ?

Yes. When?

Tomorrow good . . . ?

Sure.

Their text conversation was so devoid of emotion that he wanted to scream. He debated with himself for a moment then wrote:

Can we call . . . ?

Now? Okay.

He couldn't stop the grin overtaking his face as he phoned her. She picked up on the second ring, her voice like a breath of fresh, snow-tinged air.

"That's much better," he said.

She laughed, and he pictured her raising a hand to cover her mouth as she always did. "Not a fan of texting?"

"I don't mind it, but I feel like I don't know you well enough to understand your tone through a text. I wanted to thank you, for today. For getting Etta out of the house with me. It was fun."

"I'm glad." He heard the smile in her voice.

"What about your tree, though? Have you got one for yourself yet?"

"No." Her tone shifted—there was sadness in her words now. "I usually get one with Dylan, but I haven't asked her yet this year. She's been busy with her girlfriend, Frankie. I'm actually not sure what I'm doing for Christmas, whether I'm spending it with them or . . . by myself. It's my birthday too, so ideally, I won't be by myself." She paused. "But I'll figure it out."

Evvie spending Christmas—and *her birthday*—alone was unthinkable. "You're a Christmas baby! Well, if your friends are busy on Christmas, you could spend it with us. I know Etta would love that. And Bea and Sophie would like you."

"Oh, Matthias, you're too kind."

"I mean it." And he did. He sat up and placed the book beside him on the couch. "I know how much you love Christmas, and it's gotta be even better with your birthday! There's no way you'll be by yourself. Okay?"

She paused. "Okay. Thank you."

"Good."

They made plans to continue working on his memoir the next day, and Evvie promised to bring over ginger molasses cookies. When Matthias put down his phone, he felt pleasantly warm. He grabbed his book again but took a minute to look at the ceiling, smiling. Evvie was growing on him.

THE NEXT MORNING, Matthias and Etta pulled out a few boxes of holiday decorations from the garage. The Christmas ones were all newer since Etta had collected them after their mother had passed. They put the box with tree ornaments in the living room, then Etta took the other box to the kitchen and began decorating the house. Once the young man from the tree lot arrived with their tree, Matthias directed him to set it up in the front window. It fit perfectly in the living room, waiting to be trimmed.

Matthias had just let the man out when his phone rang. Nick's name flashed on the screen. "Hey, man," he said, answering it.

"Matty, my guy! Where've you been? You've been quiet in the chat. What's going on?"

Matthias put on another pot of coffee. "Bea and Sophie are coming over for the holidays, remember? I've been getting things ready for them." And spending time with Evvie.

But he didn't want to tell Nick about Evvie. It felt right for her to know about his band life because that was getting to know *him*, and that's what they agreed on in the first place. Telling Nick about Evvie, though . . . Matthias wanted to keep Evvie to himself for now. He didn't even want to tell Steven, although he knew Steven's reaction would be painless and maybe even congratulatory. Nick would go overboard.

"Right, yeah, you mentioned that. How's your part of the memoir coming? Steven sent his in already, the keener. Colin's been riding my ass to get mine done, but I need time to think, you know? A lot has happened since we started the band."

"We can't put *everything* in the book, Nick. Just write the important stuff."

"Ah, but see, what's important to you could be different than what's important to me. No offense, man, but my life has been a lot more exciting than yours."

And a lot more reckless, dangerous, and painful, but Matthias didn't say that. "True, true."

"You dodged the question. How's your part coming?"

"It's coming. I just need to go through it again before I send it in." That was an exaggeration and a half—he had much more work to do than that—but Nick didn't need the details. Matthias hadn't added more to the story, but he had started going through the transcription. The recording app had done a decent job of transcribing his words, but like with any technology, it wasn't perfect. He needed to go through and fix certain words, especially the names of people and places. "My goal is to send it before Christmas so I don't have to think about it during the holidays."

"Look at you, such a family man. I probably won't finish mine until New Year's Eve." Nick laughed. "Colin's gonna kill me."

Matthias rolled his eyes. He wanted to tell Nick that if he knew that, he should buckle down and work on it. But when had Nick ever listened to his advice?

"Where are you spending Christmas this year?" Matthias asked instead. Nick had a younger brother, but the two of them didn't have the best relationship. As far as Matthias knew, they hadn't spent a holiday together in decades. Nick had friends all over the world though, some of them lovers, but many of them fellow musicians or people they'd met on tour. He seemed to have no problem traveling, even now, sometimes showing up unannounced at people's houses and often outstaying his welcome. He loved people so much that he expected them to love him back the same.

"Dunno yet," Nick said. "I might crash at Carla's in New Orleans. Or maybe I'll call up Frank and see if he's free. New York is the best at Christmas."

The two of them talked about holiday plans for a few more minutes, then Matthias hung up with the excuse that he needed to finish cleaning.

Matthias and Etta had sandwiches for lunch, then Etta promised to stay out of the way when Evvie was over. "I'll be in the barn," she said. "I've got a few ideas I want to sketch out."

One o'clock came and went with no sign of Evvie, so Matthias picked up Neil Peart's book again and attempted to read. He'd been staring at the same page for ten minutes when there was a knock at the door.

"Sorry!" Evvie came inside and pulled off her boots. Matthias took her coat from her, hanging it up just like the last time she'd come over, and she handed him a container of cookies. "I was talking to Minnie and lost track of time. There's something exciting happening! I can't tell you what it is, but trust me, it's going to be fabulous!" Her eyes were sparkling, her dimples shining at full power.

"No worries," he said, putting the cookies on the table. "The kettle is boiled. Tea?"

The two of them settled at the kitchen table just like before, Matthias's phone in front of him with the transcription app set up.

Evvie glanced at the holiday centerpiece Etta had set out—three candles wrapped in red and gold plaid ribbon. Craning her neck, she looked to the living room then back to Matthias. A smile lit up her face. "The tree arrived! It looks lovely, even without trimming."

"Thanks," Matthias replied, his chest warm. "I thought we'd wait until Bea and Sophie get here to decorate it."

"I bet your granddaughter will love doing that with you."

He returned her grin. "I hope so. Now, where did we leave off?"

"You were talking about the first band you joined and how they broke up. Um . . . do you mind if I knit while you talk? I promise I'll be listening; having something to do with my hands helps me focus."

There was an innuendo in there somewhere, but Matthias ignored it for Evvie's sake. "Go for it."

Evvie pulled a blue and white garment out of the bag she'd brought with her.

"I approve of your color choice," Matthias said.

"This scarf may or may not be a gift for your sister," Evvie said. Her mouth was poised to smile. "Don't tell her."

He mimed zipping his lips. "I won't tell a soul." He went quiet, watching her knit, until she paused and looked at him. Blood rushed to his cheeks. "Oh, right. The story." How was he so distracted by watching someone *knit*? "So, after the first band I was in broke up, Etta and I both moved to California."

"Loretta went too?"

He nodded. "She moved a few months after me, and she worked in tech. I have no idea what she did, so don't ask. But she's a hell of a lot smarter than I am. She got herself set up way quicker, making money long before I was." They hadn't been as close back then, partially because he'd been jealous of her success.

He told Evvie about meeting Nick and Steven, how they'd formed Iridium Twilight and picked the name because Nick's brother was a geologist. "We thought it was clever for a rock band," he said wryly. "It was kind of a joke at first, but the name stuck."

He talked for two hours, pausing every so often so Evvie could comment on something or ask a question. She got up to refill their teas at one point, and he walked around the kitchen, stretching his leg, which had become stiff from sitting for so long.

Even though he was hitting some low points of the story—Steven's wife's cancer, Nick's drug addiction—he was comfortable. He felt like he was talking to a good friend, not to someone he'd recently met and barely knew. The way Evvie asked questions, he could tell she was truly invested, that she cared about what he had to say.

"What did Colin do when Nick got out of rehab?" Evvie asked.

"He sat the three of us down in his office, and we had a heart-to-heart. I think that's when Nick started to take everything more seriously."

"And Amy?"

Amy had been Matthias's girlfriend at the time. She'd been the one who found Nick when he overdosed in Matthias's apartment. "She left. She said it was too stressful. And I didn't blame her."

"Oh, Matthias. I'm so sorry."

"Don't be." This part of the story was harder to tell, and he didn't know if he wanted it in the memoir. He'd probably cut this piece of the transcript. "She contacted me a couple months later. She was pregnant." Evvie inhaled sharply and set her knitting in her lap. "She kept the baby, a girl. My eldest daughter, Sarah. I saw her a few times, but Amy didn't want me involved. She didn't want Sarah to get attached since I was on the road all the time." His throat thickened, and he had to stop.

Evvie was quiet, and he appreciated the space. She wasn't looking at him with pity, either. Only concern.

"Sorry," he said after a minute. He picked at a loose thread on his shirt. "I have four kids, and the only one I'm still in regular touch with is Bea." He pulled the thread all the way out, leaving a hole in his sleeve.

She reached over the table, putting her warm hand on his forearm. When he looked at her, she gave him a small smile. "It's okay," she said. "I know it must be hard."

He nodded. There was more to the story, but after all he'd said today, he didn't feel like going any further. "Speaking of Bea, do you mind if we wrap up? I need to get the spare room set up for her and Sophie."

"Oh, of course. I should get back to working on my story, anyway. I think I broke through a sticking point last night."

"Yeah? Congrats!" He went to the door with her, leaning on his cane as she laced her boots. "Would you ever let me read your story?"

She froze, her hands on her laces. She finished tying the knot then stood and grabbed her jacket from the hook on the wall. "I'm not sure," she said slowly, sliding her arms into the sleeves. "I've never let anyone read my writing before."

"Really?" Evvie seemed so open and honest, it was odd to him that she'd keep anything closed off to others. Then again, he still didn't know her very well. "Not even your best friend?"

She shook her head. "No. Dylan knows she'll get to read it eventually. I just haven't gotten the story to a place where I'm comfortable with it. I want it to be *good*, you know? Worth reading."

"Makes sense." It was similar to how he felt about his story. "You didn't ask for advice, but do you mind if I give some?"

She narrowed her eyes at him. "Tread lightly, but go ahead."

"A wonderful woman I know taught me something once. She said readers want a story to connect to, and they like messiness."

Her eyes lit up.

He continued, "She told me pressure can keep you from writing a story at all, and that could apply to feedback too. If you put too much pressure on yourself, you won't ever show someone else your work."

"Hmm." She grinned cheekily at him. "This woman sounds wonderful. I like her."

"I like her too."

The two of them were quiet, the air between them brimming with something.

Evvie bit her lip, and Matthias stepped closer to her. He felt drawn to her, as if there was a rope between them pulling them closer to each other. He was only a couple of feet away when Evvie stepped back and broke the silence.

"You know my friends from yesterday? Gem and Margie? The ones at the tree lot?"

His brow furrowed. "Yes."

"They asked me to bring you to queer seniors' night, the one I go to every Thursday. I think it could be fun if you're there, but I know Bea will have just arrived, and Hanukkah will be starting, so . . . You don't have to come."

His heart skipped a beat. "You're . . . queer?"

"I am, yes. Is that alright?" She raised her chin slightly as if she expected to defend herself.

"Of course!" He pushed as much assurance into his voice as he could. Her openness with him, and the revelation that she was queer, filled him with new energy. "I am too, sort of. I . . . it's a long story." At her questioning look, he waved a hand. "We can talk about it later." And he wanted to, he really did. He didn't have many queer friends other than Etta. "But . . . you're inviting me to a queer seniors' group?"

"Yes? Unless you don't want to come." Her eyes fell on those words, and he couldn't stand to see her frown like that.

"I would love to go with you."

"Really?"

"Really."

Evvie shifted from foot to foot. "Great! But um . . . my friends think we're dating."

She looked at him, not saying anything, and he wasn't sure how he was supposed to react. At least if they thought he and Evvie were dating, she probably wasn't a lesbian, which boded well for his feelings. "Oh?" He hooked a thumb through his beltloop.

"I kind of didn't dispel the notion." At this, he raised his eyebrows. Evvie continued, "Part of what I'm struggling with in my book is to see how others react to the main couple. I have experience from an outside perspective, obviously, but . . ."

Ah, yes. Her book. "But you want to experience it as someone *in* the couple."

"Yes." Her cheeks were flaming red.

He ran a hand over his beard. This was taking their deal one step further—fake dating around people they knew. Or, at least, people Evvie knew. It was just as ridiculous, but the chance to act as Evvie's actual partner intrigued him. He wondered if she hadn't "dispelled the notion" because it intrigued her, too. "Let's do it. It could be fun."

She let out a breath. "Okay. I'll pick you up at six fifteen on Thursday then."

"Sounds good."

He took another step closer to her, curious to see if the kiss on the cheek yesterday had been a fluke. Throughout their entire conversation, the tension in the air hadn't dissipated. If anything, it had gotten stronger. He leaned toward her, slowly, and the corners of her lips twitched. He tilted his head, giving her easy access to his cheek.

She stood on her tiptoes just as slowly and pressed her lips to his face. They were soft against his beard. When she pulled back, she was smirking.

"I'll see you on Thursday," she said, and he could have sworn there was a skip in her step as she headed to her car.

He felt lighter, too, for the rest of that day. And he couldn't stop thinking about Evvie.

CHAPTER SEVENTEEN

EVVIE

*A*t six thirty on Thursday, Evvie knocked on Matthias and Loretta's door. She'd been a ball of anxiety for the past day and a half, and she was glad they were finally going on their fake date to meet her friends. A few more hours, and she'd have called the whole thing off.

A patter of footsteps came from the other side of the door, then it opened to reveal a little girl wearing a bright green tutu and a matching top, her brown hair in a French braid. She stared at Evvie with wide brown eyes, and Evvie's anxiety eased.

Tilting her head, the girl asked, "Who are you?"

Evvie smiled. "My name is Evvie. Are you Sophie?"

The girl nodded.

"I'm friends with your grandpa and your Aunt Etta. Do you know where they are?" She leaned to peer around Sophie, but there were no adults in sight.

"Catching a chicken," Sophie said matter-of-factly.

"Catching a chicken?"

"Mm-hmm." Sophie turned on her heel and ran inside, leaving the door wide open.

"Alrighty then." Evvie stepped inside and closed the door

behind her. No one came to greet her, and Sophie settled at the coffee table in the living room, her head bent over a coloring book. Evvie slipped off her boots and went to sit by Sophie on the couch.

"What are you coloring?" she asked.

"Sharks," Sophie answered. "See?" She held up her coloring page, which was indeed a picture of cartoonish sharks. "Want to color with me?"

Evvie smiled. "I'd love to." It would give her something to occupy herself with until Matthias came in. She lowered herself carefully to the floor and stuck her legs under the table as Sophie passed her a coloring page of a seahorse.

Sophie was telling her how badly she wanted a dog when the back door creaked open and Matthias, Loretta, and a younger woman who must have been Bea filed inside.

"Evvie!" Matthias said. "Shit, sorry. We had an escapee to catch."

"Dad, language." Bea swatted his arm. The resemblance between her and Sophie was striking; they had the same round face, wide brown eyes, and thick eyelashes. There was a trace of Matthias there too, in the shape of her mouth and the set of her eyebrows.

"Sorry," Matthias replied, cringing.

Evvie pushed herself to stand, her knees cracking. "Can I finish this another day?" she asked Sophie, gesturing to the barely colored seahorse. Sophie nodded. "Thank you. Keep it safe for me, okay?" At this, Sophie nodded again solemnly and slid the paper into the front of her coloring book.

Evvie walked over to Matthias as she brushed off her leggings. "Sophie told me you were chasing a chicken?"

Loretta crossed her arms, but a smile stole over her lips. "Yes, a little explorer didn't close the door properly when she visited the goddesses earlier. Athena got loose."

"And she didn't want to be caught," Bea added, pushing hair out of her eyes. It was braided like Sophie's, but the braid was falling out, likely from the chicken chase. "I'm Bea." She held out her hand.

Evvie shook it and introduced herself. "It's wonderful to meet you. Sophie welcomed me in."

"I swear, she doesn't normally let strangers in the house," Bea said. "She knew to expect you."

Evvie laughed, her hand over her mouth. "I'm not judging, don't worry."

"We need to get going, don't we?" Matthias asked, looking at the clock on the wall.

"Oh! Goodness, we do," Evvie said.

She had just finished putting her boots on when there was a knock at the door.

Loretta, who had sat in the recliner to sketch, looked up with furrowed eyebrows. "Are you expecting anyone?" she asked Matthias.

"No," he said, frowning. "And you clearly aren't either."

"Don't look at me," Bea said from the kitchen, where she was making hot chocolate.

Matthias went to the door and looked through the peephole. Whoever he saw on the other side made him inhale sharply and squeeze his eyes shut.

Evvie braced herself as he pulled the door open.

"Hey, man!"

Leaning slightly to one side, Evvie could see a man standing there with a carry-on suitcase at his feet, wearing a sweater much too thin for Canadian winters and thick-rimmed black glasses. He looked to be about their age, his tanned skin wrinkled. There was something more worn about him, though, and his short silver hair was thinning. "Happy Hanukkah!"

"Nick," Matthias said, the enthusiasm in his voice sounding slightly forced. "What are you doing here?"

"You're not gonna invite me in first? I'm freezing my ass off here."

"Sorry, come in, come in." He stepped aside, and Evvie stepped back to make room.

Nick came in, shaking his limbs as if he could shake off the cold. "Hello," he said to Evvie. "And who might you be?"

"Um." Evvie shifted uncomfortably. "I'm Evvie, a . . . a friend of Matthias's."

"A *friend*, hey?" Nick waggled his eyebrows, and Evvie's face went hot. "Matty, my man!" He slapped Matthias's arm. "You sly dog, you! You didn't tell me you had a girlfriend." While Matthias stammered something about Evvie being just a friend, Nick held out his hand to Evvie. She put hers out warily; he took it and kissed it as if he were a knight and she a princess.

Then he moved on to address the rest of the room. "Etta, there's my girl!"

"Nick," she said, her tone verging on scolding. "What are you doing here?"

"Why does everyone ask me that?" Nick rubbed his hands together. "Hey, Bea. Sophie, is that you? You've grown an entire foot since I saw you last!" Sophie's eyes nearly took up her entire face, and Evvie got the feeling she had no clue who Nick was.

"Hi, Nick," Bea said, her tone slightly exasperated.

"Nick, can I talk to you for a minute?" Matthias said before Nick could make things more awkward.

"Sure, what's up?"

Matthias grabbed Nick's arm and dragged him toward his room. "Whoa, hey, watch it," Nick said. "This is a designer sweater."

As they disappeared out of sight, Evvie flapped her arms at her sides. "Should I take my boots off again?"

Bea looked at her with sympathy. "Maybe."

CHAPTER EIGHTEEN

MATTHIAS

*M*atthias ignored Nick's protest about his sweater; Nick didn't pay attention to who designed his clothes, no matter what he said.

"You never answered my question," Matthias said once they were in his room, forcing himself to speak quietly. "What are you doing here?"

Nick leaned toward him as if about to reveal a secret. "I called both Carla and Frank, and neither of them answered. So I sent them messages online. Still, nothing. So I reached out to a couple more people . . . It's like everyone's disappeared. Poof! Off the map. I didn't want to spend Christmas alone or in some hotel with people I didn't know, and I didn't want to go to Steven's 'cause he's got like six grandkiddos, so I thought I'd pop up here and visit you. Surprise!"

Matthias had the feeling Carla, Frank, and whoever else Nick had contacted had not answered for a reason. And that reason was currently standing in front of him. "I'm definitely surprised," he said.

"You don't mind putting me up for a couple weeks, do you?"

Hell yes, he minded. But what Nick had said . . . he didn't want to spend Christmas alone. How could Matthias say no to him staying? "I don't mind," he said. "But you really should have called first. This is Etta's place more than mine, and you know how she feels about unexpected things."

Nick rubbed the back of his neck. "Yeah, sorry. I forgot. I won't get in the way, though, I swear. You'll barely know I'm here."

Matthias rolled his eyes. "Sure, sure."

"So you've got a girlfriend? Matty boy, why didn't you tell me?"

Fuck. There was no way Matthias could go to the queer seniors' night with Evvie now; he wouldn't leave Etta and Bea to wrangle Nick.

"I need to go talk to Evvie. Stay here." He sighed, opening the door. Shrugging, Nick settled on Matthias's bed.

As soon as Matthias entered the living room, both Bea and Etta got up to meet him, quietly hissing questions about Nick. He relayed the situation to them. "I'm sorry, I had no idea he would do this. Listen, I'll tell him to stay in my room, and I'll try to keep him busy. He's not that bad all the time. Maybe it'll even be fun to have him here for the holidays."

Etta looked about ready to murder someone. "If he calls me *my girl* one more time, he's sleeping in the barn."

That was fair. "Noted."

"This should be interesting," Bea said, going to sit beside Sophie on the floor.

Evvie sat on the couch, her face red, gazing out the window. Matthias went over to her and touched her shoulder lightly. "Can we talk? Outside maybe?"

She nodded and put her boots and coat on without a word. They went out back, sitting on the bench against the house beside the chicken coop. The chickens were currently warming up inside, so there wasn't much to see.

"So, that's Nick," Evvie said.

"That's Nick. He can be . . . a lot, but he's a good guy. I had no idea he was coming, but this is exactly the kind of stunt he likes to pull. I think he thought I'd be happy to see him."

Evvie looked at him, her chin tucked into the collar of her jacket. "You're not?"

He shook his head. "Not really. Etta doesn't like Nick much, and I was enjoying the quiet. The word *quiet* isn't even in Nick's vocabulary."

Evvie made a low humming noise. "And you won't turn him away?"

"He said that if he wasn't here, he'd be spending Christmas alone or in a hotel with people he doesn't know. To be honest, that would be entirely his own fault. But . . ."

"But you're a good friend," Evvie said.

"That's one way to put it." They sat without speaking for a couple minutes, looking past the chicken coop to the yard and the trees beyond. Matthias cleared his throat. "I won't be able to come tonight."

"I know. You've got a friend to entertain now."

"I'm sorry." He grabbed Evvie's gloved hand, giving it a little squeeze.

"It's not your fault," she said. "I think I should go. Let you figure things out with Nick."

He sighed. "I'll call you tomorrow?"

"Yes, please." She kissed his cheek, filling his chest with warmth, and walked around the house to her car, probably not wanting to go back inside and risk running into Nick again.

He stayed outside for a few minutes then went back in. He glanced around, and Etta said, "He's still in your room." At least Nick had listened to him this time.

He made two cups of coffee—one for himself and one for Nick—and carried them to his room carefully, using his cane to knock on the door.

"Took you long enough," Nick said brightly as he opened the door. "Oh, god bless you," he said, taking a cup of coffee from Matthias.

Matthias settled on the bed beside him, his knee complaining. "Listen, Nick. If you're going to stay here for the holidays, you've gotta follow some ground rules."

Nick nodded solemnly as he sipped his coffee.

"No referring to Etta as *my girl*." Nick went to say something, but Matthias held up a hand. "No protests, these are the rules. No referring to Etta as *my girl*," he repeated more firmly. "No swearing around Sophie. No getting drunk. And for fuck's sake, be careful about who sees you. I don't need people knowing where I live, got it?"

Nick waved him off. "Yeah, yeah, I got it. Everything will be fine."

Even though Nick said that, he looked shifty-eyed. Matthias sighed. "What did you do?"

"Nothing," Nick said, widening his eyes. "I might have taken a selfie with some kid at the airport, but—"

"Seriously? Shit." Matthias shook his head. Of course someone would recognize Nick at the airport.

"Listen, the kid was *departing*, okay? He didn't follow me here or anything."

Matthias clenched his jaw. "You better hope not."

They were quiet for a moment, and the tension between them dissipated. When Matthias looked at Nick again, his expression had softened. "Thanks for letting me stay here."

Matthias rubbed a hand over his face and hoped Nick would truly behave himself. If it were just the two of them, they'd have fun together no doubt, but Matthias was with his family. The last thing he wanted was a chaotic holiday season.

CHAPTER NINETEEN

EVVIE

$\mathcal{M}$eeting Nick hadn't been the most pleasant experience, and Evvie could see why Loretta might not like him. He'd barged in unannounced, taking Matthias for granted. Assuming Matthias would welcome him, which of course, Matthias had.

But the part that bothered Evvie the most was how they'd had to cancel their fake date.

Even though Evvie understood why, her anxiety poked at her, whispering, *You don't mean that much to him. You aren't important. He picked Nick over you.*

She did her best to shut the voice up, but it didn't seem to work even though she was sure she'd taken her anxiety medication *and* her ADHD medication. Her thoughts swirled so much that she almost didn't go to queer seniors' night.

And once she got there, she wished she'd stayed home. Gem had obviously told everyone about Matthias because they asked where Matthias was, why he wasn't with her. She pasted a smile on her face and told them the truth, minus the part that Nick was the lead singer of Iridium Twilight.

Although she wasn't feeling the best, her friends' interest in Matthias was somewhat reassuring; clearly, they didn't think her dating a man made her any less queer. Part of her knew her insecurity was ridiculous when it came to her group, but being bi and dating the opposite gender could be a real concern elsewhere in the queer community. People weren't as loving as you hoped they'd be all the time.

For the rest of the evening, she couldn't focus, her thoughts bouncing from Nick to Matthias, to her ex-husband, to her manuscript, to the card game she was supposed to be playing. For the first time ever, she left early, claiming she had a headache—which wasn't a lie.

Evvie slept horribly that night, and she woke up on Friday feeling disgusting. Even a wonderfully sugary breakfast of Cinnamon Toast Crunch didn't cheer her up. She got dressed, keeping her phone with her, watching the screen and willing Matthias to call her. If he didn't soon, she'd have to go out and do something to distract herself.

When her phone finally went off, it was a text instead of a call. It was Matthias, though, and the two of them made plans to meet the next day, Saturday. Matthias's texts were more to-the-point than usual, and she suspected he was with Nick and didn't have time to type more.

With nothing else to do, Evvie dove into revisions of her story and spent the rest of the day puttering around, looking forward to seeing Matthias.

BUT SATURDAY CAME, and she still hadn't heard from him by noon. She phoned him, knowing he preferred it to texting, even if he'd done nothing but text the day before.

"Hey," he answered. She could hear Sophie laughing in the background and a low voice that was probably Nick's. "I'm sorry I didn't phone you. I've been a bit busy."

"It's alright. What's today looking like?" Their plans hadn't been set in stone, but they said they'd get together, probably work on the band memoir. They could go for a walk after to see the Christmas lights, maybe even with Matthias's family.

Matthias sighed. "Today isn't going to work. Nick wants to go to Vancouver, and if I don't go with him, he'll probably end up all over tomorrow's tabloids."

Evvie swallowed her disappointment. "Well, today's plans weren't concrete anyway."

"I know, but still. I'll let you know as soon as we can get together, okay?" She knew he meant getting together to work on the memoir, but it felt like he meant more than that. Like he was saying *I'll let you know as soon as we can go on a date*. It was probably her wishful thinking.

"Do you think Monday will work? Queer seniors' night changed days next week because of a scheduling conflict." Her heart was in her throat as she waited for his answer. He'd missed the last meeting, and he'd canceled today's plans. She felt fragile in the face of another possible missed date.

He hesitated then said, "Screw it, I don't care what Nick decides to do on Monday. I'll be there."

A smile stole over her face, her spirits lifting slightly at his answer. *Take that, anxiety.* Monday wasn't that far away. Only two days until her next fake date.

Once they hung up, though, her anxiety rushed back. What if Monday came around and Nick wanted to do something else, and Matthias caved and canceled last minute again? Evvie didn't want to be alone with her thoughts, so she invited Dylan and Frankie over to play board games and take her mind off things.

"So, what have you learned about Iridium Twilight?" Dylan said, lightly digging an elbow into Evvie's ribs after she took off her coat. So much for taking her mind off Matthias.

"Nothing I can tell you," Evvie replied. Should she tell Dylan about Nick being in town? It'd probably get out eventually, so she didn't see the harm in it. When Evvie described how Nick had shown up out of the blue, Dylan gasped.

"Nick's here?" Dylan grabbed Frankie's arm but dropped it

immediately and tried to play it cool. "Frankie, Nick Evans is in town," she said, as if she barely cared.

"You don't say," Frankie said, laughing.

"Do you think . . . could you maybe get me an autograph from him too?" Dylan asked Evvie.

Evvie raised an eyebrow. "Maybe." She didn't feel much like talking to Nick right now, but she might be more amenable on Monday.

Small talk and news aside, the three of them sat at Evvie's kitchen table with a game called Cascadia. "I haven't seen this one before," Dylan said. "Is it new?" She lifted one of the hexagonal pieces and examined it.

Evvie nodded. "Hijiri recommended it to me. He said it's not too difficult, but it's challenging enough that we'll enjoy it." Hijiri owned Tabletop Time, the board game store on Main Street.

"How do you play?" Frankie asked. "Fair warning, I haven't played many board games before. If you want to play cards, though, I know more games than I can count."

Dylan poured them wine while Evvie explained the game, and once they got going, it was fun like Hijiri had said. There was something soothing about matching landscapes and making animal groupings, although Evvie's anxiety still sat just below the surface.

"Can we play again?" Frankie asked after Dylan won. "I think I understand it better now. And I need to beat Dylan this time."

Dylan smirked. "More wine first," she said, topping up their glasses.

Evvie laid out a new line of tiles and started the game. She was starting to feel antsy, which was unusual when she drank wine. While Frankie took her turn, Evvie put on the kettle; maybe a cup of tea would help.

When Dylan's turn came, she stared at the tiles, her forehead creased in thought. Evvie bit her lip, willing Dylan to pick a tile. She was enjoying the game, but it wasn't supposed to take this long. Dylan tapped her fingernails on the table and pursed her lips, still staring.

"Jiminy Christmas, Dylan, will you just pick a darn tile?" Evvie snapped, the words out of her mouth before she knew it.

Dylan looked at Evvie over her reading glasses, her eyebrows raised, and Frankie shot Evvie a look. "What was that?" Frankie asked.

Evvie scrunched her eyes shut. "I'm sorry. I don't know what came over me, but that was uncalled for."

"I have never seen you snap at someone," Frankie said.

"That's because Evvie doesn't usually snap." Dylan gave Evvie a concerned look. "Are you okay, Ev?"

Evvie really wasn't feeling herself in that moment, and she got up to pace in front of the sink. "I've just been a little . . . on edge today." They already knew about Nick, but now she told them about how Nick's appearance had spoiled her plans with Matthias. Twice. "I feel foolish for being upset about this."

"You're not foolish," Dylan said, and Frankie nodded. "You were looking forward to spending time with Matthias, and now you have to wait even longer to see him. That sucks."

"I suppose." Evvie returned to her chair with a sigh.

"This Nick guy doesn't sound like the most considerate person, either," Frankie said. She tilted her head toward Dylan. "Even if you like him as a singer."

"No, I know." Dylan folded her hands on the table. "He's always been kind of wild. Which I like reading about in the news, but it's not fun when it affects my best friend."

Evvie gave her a small smile. She appreciated her friends' support and validation, but she didn't want to think about Nick or Matthias anymore. "For the rest of the evening, let's not talk about any members of Iridium Twilight." She tapped the table. "I do believe it's your turn, Dylan."

MONDAY SEEMED to take forever to arrive, but finally it did. When Evvie went to pick up Matthias for queer seniors' night, Nick opened the door. "Hey, Matthias's not-girlfriend!" he said in greeting. Evvie's face heated, and he continued, "Kidding, kidding, come on in." He gestured her inside like he owned the place.

"Hi, Evvie," Bea said from the couch. She was shaking her head at Nick, but the gesture seemed good natured, unlike her attitude toward him when he'd first arrived.

"Ready to go?" Matthias asked, coming around the corner. He wore jeans and a cozy brown sweater, perfect for a casual night out. Evvie was torn in two, part of her wanting to admire how the sweater sat on Matthias's shoulders, and another part of her almost hyperventilating at the thought that she'd lied to her friends about dating Matthias.

For research, she reminded herself.

A few minutes later, she and Matthias were in her car. She'd hoped being with him would calm her, but nausea took over as soon as she buckled her seatbelt.

"I don't know if I can do this," she said, placing her hands on the wheel but keeping the car in park.

"What? Are you okay?" Matthias turned to her. "We don't have to go if you're not feeling well."

"I'm not sick, I just . . . I need a distraction. I'm sure I'll be fine in a minute." Distractions seemed high on her priority list lately. She cracked her window slightly to let in the fresh, cold air. "Want to tell more of your story on the way?"

He paused for a moment as she turned the car around. "Actually, can we talk about this whole"—he gestured between the two of them—"queer thing for a minute?"

"Of course." That was a topic that could hold her attention.

"So . . . I don't really identify as anything." His words were stilted, as if he didn't talk about this often. "I've been attracted to men at times, but in the circles I moved in, being gay wasn't really accepted. Not openly, anyway. Nowadays, people like Elton John and David Bowie have huge followings, and a lot of glam rock is more mainstream. It wasn't like that when my career was growing. That stuff was countercultural.

"Anyway, when I was in my late thirties, I started seeing a man, sort of. We weren't really together, but we were getting to know each other. I went to a gay club with him, but Colin found out somehow." He paused, seeming to search for words. "He asked me not to go there anymore. Said the publicity would be bad for the band. So I didn't. I stopped spending time with my friend, we went our separate ways . . . I never went to another gay club."

"Oh, Matthias." Evvie's heart hurt for him.

"I haven't felt comfortable with being . . . queer, as you say, since then. It's something I've known about myself this whole time, but not something I've been able to embrace. So, you asking me to come with you . . . it means a lot."

Tears pricked Evvie's eyes, and she blinked them away so she could see the road clearly. "I'm glad." She reached for his hand, grasping it tightly when he took it. "This group is a safe space. We don't use the word *queer* there, though, just so you know. I'm fine with it, but some of my friends aren't. The official group title is the LGBTQ+ Seniors' Group."

"I can understand that."

She glanced at him, his expression saying, *I see you. I understand you. We're in this together.* She hoped her expression said the same.

It was only after they'd been quiet for a minute that her anxiety flooded in again. She pulled her hand to the steering wheel. "So, um, I know you were just talking, but do you want to talk more? About the band?"

"Okay," he said. He pulled up the recording app and put his phone in the cup holder. As he spoke and his story gained rhythm, a wave of calm washed over Evvie. His low voice was familiar now, comforting. She focused on his story as much as she could. He told her about touring, what life was like on the tour bus. About the fans and how Colin had increased security because of a few "incidents."

The longer he spoke, the more Evvie had to force herself to listen and not drown in her own thoughts. She'd gone back and forth with herself over the past few days—was it okay to lie to her friends about dating Matthias?

On one hand, she hadn't told them she and Matthias were dating. She merely hadn't corrected Gem's assumption.

There was *something* between them, even if neither of them had acknowledged it. Yet. Pretending to be together could be fun! Not to mention this was about research for her novel, about discovering what it was like to date someone, so the whole plan would be ruined if her friends knew they *weren't* dating.

But lying had always made Evvie sick, and lying by omission was no exception. After tonight, she'd have to tell everyone she and Matthias broke up. There was no way she could keep up the charade.

They pulled into the community center parking lot. "Poor timing," Matthias said. "I was just about to tell you about my knee."

"On the way home, maybe?"

He reached out and grabbed her hand, and her heart jumped into her throat. "Are you okay? I have a feeling you didn't hear most of what I said for the second half of the drive."

She groaned and pulled away from him to put her face in her hands. "I'm sorry," she said, her voice muffled. "My brain is all over the place right now. More than usual." In moments like this, she wondered if her medication did anything at all.

There was warm pressure on her shoulder—his hand. "It's okay," he said. "Do you still want to go inside?"

She straightened, breathing deeply. "Yes," she said firmly. "Let's do it." She wasn't about to take this away from him, not after how he'd confided in her. "You are my boyfriend, and I am your girlfriend. Fudge nuggets, scratch that." She hated how heterosexual the words *boyfriend* and *girlfriend* sounded when paired together. "We are partners. Yes, partners. Right? For tonight?"

"Yes. For tonight." There was a spark of something in his eyes, but she didn't have enough mental energy to think about it.

Once out of the car, they clasped hands, and she tried not to crush his fingers as they went inside.

The main hall of the community center looked completely different than usual. There was still a table set up for snacks and drinks, but it held a giant bowl of popcorn with two smaller bowls beside it. There was no circle of chairs. Instead, a few comfy chairs and couches faced the bare wall, where the title screen for *Under the Christmas Tree* was projected. Gem sat in the chair closest to them, Tom and Noah were cuddling in a loveseat, and Priya sat in a recliner.

"Good evening," Gem said, getting up to greet them. "Matthias, it's nice to see you."

Matthias let go of Evvie's hand to shake Gem's, and Evvie resisted the urge to snatch it back. Since when had she relied on someone else for security? She lifted her chin and pushed her shoulder blades together, trying to regain her dignity.

Priya came over to join them. "So *you're* the Matthias we've been hearing about. You sure know how to pick 'em, Evvie," she said with a wink.

Evvie laughed, but it sounded horribly forced. "I do, don't I?"

"We're glad to have you here, Matthias." Gem gestured at the others. "This is Priya, and over there are Tom and Noah." The two men waved at Matthias, who waved back. "I thought we'd have a movie night for something different."

"And there's popcorn!" Priya added. "I even brought different salts so you can spice it up."

Gem led them to the table. "Let's get you a movie snack."

Evvie's heart pounded as she and Matthias grabbed bowls of popcorn. The two of them walked over to the couches, and Evvie was about to sit on the empty one at the back when Gem said, "Matthias, are you okay to come up here for a minute? Since it's your first time here, I thought we'd all share a fun fact about ourselves. We did highs and lows earlier, so you can add yours too if you want."

"Oh, okay."

Evvie took Matthias's popcorn bowl and practically collapsed onto the couch as he went up front to stand with Gem. Things were going well so far, but Evvie wasn't feeling much better about the scenario.

"I'll go first," Gem said. "A fun fact about me is that I've been skydiving in Switzerland."

"Have you really?" Tom asked. "What made you do that?"

Gem shrugged. "What can I say? I like adrenaline rushes. Tom, you next."

Tom shared that he used to professionally build treehouses, then Noah told them he had no family in Canada—they all lived in Nigeria. Priya's fun fact was that she kept a collection of handwritten letters from a lover she had in her twenties.

"Your turn, Evvie." Gem motioned to her. "Matthias can go last."

Evvie sat up straighter and blurted the first story that came to her mind. "One time, back when I worked at the vet clinic, I forgot to put away a blood vial before I left. It was in my pocket. I did laundry that night, and the vial broke. It looked like a murder scene."

She didn't know if it was her delivery or the story itself, but no one laughed. Tom said, "Oh my," and Gem stared at her with raised eyebrows.

"That sounds like a mess." Matthias was the only one grinning. "My turn, then? Fun fact about me . . . I used to be in a band, and when I was fifty-seven, I jumped off an amp and shattered my left knee cap." Everyone winced, and Priya groaned. "Thank goodness it was my left one. I'm a drummer and I'm right-handed, so if it had been the right one, that could have been a problem. That's why I use a cane."

"It's not that odd, though, is it?" Noah said. "Someone using a cane at our age."

Matthias shrugged. "I guess not."

He came to sit beside Evvie, choosing the middle cushion right beside her rather than the farther one. Once his cane was safely leaning beside him, Evvie handed him his popcorn. She was surprised Matthias had given out so much information about himself, but she was glad he was that comfortable with her friends.

Priya leaned around her chair to look at them. "We should have asked how you two met."

Evvie froze like she had at the tree lot, but Matthias didn't miss a beat. He put his hand on her thigh, just above her knee. "We met at the bakery in Juniper Creek. I spilled my coffee all over her, actually."

Heat shot up Evvie's thigh from his hand, and she tried not to react to it. "I spilled my coffee all over him as well." Telling the truth about how they'd met eased the tightness in her chest. "I'm afraid I ruined the perfectly nice sweater he was wearing."

He squeezed her leg lightly. "But it was worth it, hey? Look at us now." He moved his hand, putting his arm around her shoulders and drawing her in close.

Now *this* she could get used to. If they hadn't been faking a relationship, she didn't think she'd have the courage to do what she did next. She snuggled against him, breathing in his pine scent.

"Well, isn't that cute," Noah said, reminding Evvie that there were other people in the room. Priya wasn't the only one looking at them now—everyone was staring at them, all of them smiling.

Evvie couldn't decide if their approval made her feel better or worse.

Finally, Gem got to her feet. "Let's get this show on the road, shall we?" She went and flicked off the lights, then she started the movie.

CHAPTER TWENTY

MATTHIAS

*E*ven though Evvie had cuddled up to Matthias, she felt stiff beneath his arm. She clutched her popcorn bowl between her hands like it was about to fly off on its own, and she hadn't even undone her jacket.

As the movie began, he rubbed his hand up and down her arm, leaning closer to whisper, "Relax. Everything is going well, and this seems like your kind of movie."

She looked up at him, the light from the screen reflecting in her eyes. "I'll try," she whispered back.

After the first few movie scenes stuffed full of Christmas cheer, Evvie softened against him. Her shoulders relaxed, and she popped a few pieces of popcorn into her mouth. Minutes later, she leaned forward to take off her jacket. Matthias helped her, and she settled against him again.

He pulled her closer, enjoying the warmth of her body. In the movie, two women who both adored Christmas fell in love surrounded by stockings, jingle bells, wreaths, lights, reindeer antlers, and snow. It was a Christmas lover's dream, and Matthias heard Evvie sigh more than once as the women made heart eyes at each other.

When Evvie finished her popcorn, she set the bowl aside and shifted so she was lying against Matthias's chest. She draped an arm over his stomach and leaned her head against him. The position was so cozy, so *loving*, that he couldn't help but lean down and brush a kiss on top of her head. Her arm moved slightly—not quite a squeeze—but she didn't react otherwise.

Matthias struggled to watch the movie after that, his attention on Evvie and how comfortable he was with her. He'd experienced moments like this a few times with Bea's mom, Hannah, but this seemed lower pressure somehow.

He and Evvie weren't dating. There were no expectations for either of them in this scenario, and yet they'd chosen to sit this way. To be near each other just because they enjoyed it. They were at the back of the room and none of Evvie's friends could see them without effort, so it wasn't even for show.

As the movie ended, Evvie breathed deeply, holding him the slightest bit tighter. She tilted her head and whispered, "I don't want to move."

"Me either," he said, wrapping his other arm around her so she was enclosed comfortably against him.

He could easily see the two of them like this at home on the couch, watching TV. Or in bed, listening to music or just waking up.

Waking up together.

He cleared his throat and shifted as he swelled against his jeans. Now was *not* the time for this—not when Evvie was practically on top of him, and Gem was about to turn the lights on. As he moved, Evvie made a quiet whine in the back of her throat, which only made him harder.

"Is there a bathroom here?" he asked quietly, trying to be gentle about moving her.

She sat up, finally. "Down the hall," she said, pointing. He grabbed his cane and went to the bathroom, glad he'd found a way to collect himself.

A few minutes later, he emerged back into the hall to find everyone standing around, talking. Evvie had her jacket on again, her face slightly flushed. "Ready to go?"

Matthias nodded and said goodbye to everyone. Gem said he was welcome to come again, and Priya added, "Yes, please do," in a suggestive voice.

He and Evvie held hands on their way to the car once more, neither of them saying a word. He'd give his favorite drumsticks to know what was going through her head in that moment.

Once they were both settled in the car, he asked, "So? How do you think that went?"

She combed her fingers through her hair, looking forward rather than at him. "Good, I think. Did you enjoy yourself?"

He did, but not in the way she was asking. "Yeah, yeah. The movie was kind of cheesy."

That caught her attention, and she snapped her gaze to his. "It was cute!" she said indignantly. "And gay! Can't ask for more, in my opinion."

He laughed. "It was cute. And gay. Pretty formulaic, though."

She scoffed. "Of course it was. It's a romcom. They're all formulaic, but that's why people like them. And it's about time the queer community got some good ones."

"You're not wrong."

They were quiet again as they started toward Juniper Creek.

"Do you want to continue your story?" Evvie asked once they were on the highway. There weren't many cars out that evening.

"No. I do want to talk, though."

"Oh?" Evvie glanced at him.

"You seemed nervous earlier about the whole fake-dating thing. How do you feel about it now?"

She didn't answer for a minute, and he was sure she was chewing the inside of her cheek. Finally, she said, "It wasn't as bad as I expected." When she glanced at him again, her expression was coy. "It was kind of fun, actually."

"Yeah?"

"Yes. You're a good movie-watching buddy."

Movie-watching buddy. Was that truly what she thought? He suspected it wasn't, and he definitely wanted to be more than that to her.

"Should we go again next week?" he asked.

"Hmm. I don't know. I don't really want to keep this up."

He hesitated. "Keep *what* up?"

She sighed. "The lie that we're dating. While it was fun, and useful for my research"—he held back a laugh—"faking it makes me feel unwell."

"Makes sense." He knew exactly what he wanted to say next, but he waited for them to pull up in front of the house. He had an idea of how Evvie would react to his statement, but he wanted them stationary first, just in case.

"Walk me to the door?" he said once they parked. He wanted to see her under the porch light so he could gauge her expression better. So he could see her beautiful blue eyes.

"Sure."

They got out and made their way up the front steps. He stopped in front of the door and stood to face her. "What if it wasn't fake?" he asked.

"Sorry, what?" Her eyebrows drew together, and she tucked a strand of hair behind her ear. "What do you mean?"

Her eyes were bright, even in the dark, and he had the urge to touch her cheek. But he'd wait.

He focused on keeping his breathing slow; this moment carried much more weight than he'd expected. If she said no . . . He'd be okay. He'd still want to be friends with her, to work on their stories together. But it would also break his heart.

He'd never fallen this fast before, and it scared him. He didn't have the best track record when it came to relationships.

"What if our relationship wasn't fake?" he asked. "What if it was real?"

Evvie's lips parted—not in a jaw drop, but in a soft sigh of surprise. "Are you . . . asking me on a date?"

He laughed lightly through his nose. "Not quite. We've been on a few of those already, haven't we? I'm asking if you'll be my partner."

"Oh." She blinked a few times, her gaze elsewhere, then she focused back on him. "You want to go steady? To be exclusive?" He nodded, and her eyes were wider than he'd ever seen them. "Well, that would certainly make it easier . . . You know, to tell the truth instead of lying about dating." A realization seemed to wash over her. "What am I saying? Of course, Matthias." She stepped forward and grabbed his free hand. "I'd love to."

He leaned his cane against the door then pulled her closer, his hand on her face. Her soft skin was cold from the chilly December air. He brushed his thumb along her cheekbone, smiling when she leaned into his palm.

Leaning forward, he brought his face toward hers, slowly, giving her plenty of room to back out.

She didn't.

Their lips pressed together, and he brought his other hand to her face so he could hold her there, learning how she moved, what she liked.

When he pulled back for air, she surged forward, crushing her lips to his once again. He fell against the door frame, and they both laughed as she helped him straighten.

"Sorry," she said sheepishly. "Too much enthusiasm."

He quirked a brow. "Or not enough."

They kissed again, gently this time. He wanted to savor the taste of her, the way she fisted her hands in his jacket.

He paused to look at her, and she gasped, looking beyond him. "Oh," she said, her entire face lighting up. "It's snowing!"

She was right. Fat, fluffy snowflakes drifted down around them, landing on their hair. One of them blew onto Evvie's eyelashes, and she laughed; it was the first time he'd seen her laugh without covering her mouth.

She let go of Matthias and ran down the stairs with her arms outstretched. Still lit by the porch light, she spun in a circle, her head tilted back, giggling like Sophie had earlier that day with the chickens.

Matthias grinned so wide it hurt his cheeks.

It was a perfect December night.

CHAPTER TWENTY-ONE

EVVIE

To top off their perfect evening, Matthias invited Evvie inside to light the menorah and say the blessings with everyone. She could hardly believe he'd asked her to go steady, and now, to participate in something so personal with his family. Despite their kisses and the lightness in her chest, she was nervous, having never celebrated Hanukkah before. But she needn't have worried.

Everyone was wearing the Hanukkah sweaters Matthias had gotten at the market, and they turned out the lights and stood in front of the window while Bea lit the candles and sang the prayers in Hebrew. Etta brought out a plate of latkes, complete with bowls of sour cream and applesauce, which surprisingly worked best combined on the latke in a single bite. As Evvie munched, Sophie showed her and Nick how to play dreidel, spinning the top and collecting gelt from the pile depending which letter the dreidel landed on. It was an honor that Matthias let her into his life this way, that she got to see him in his element with his family.

Before Evvie drove home, they organized a meeting on Saturday so Matthias could continue his story, although the two of them planning to get together had an entirely different feeling now. They kissed again in the snow, and Evvie almost cried with joy.

Everything she wished for was coming true. She'd found someone to be with over the holidays and on her birthday, her novel was coming along, her friends were all happy, and it was snowing. The satisfaction brimming in her chest surpassed what she'd felt when she finally retired.

She wasn't only free now—she was free, and happy, and loved in all the ways she wanted to be.

THE NEXT MORNING, she was still riding that high when she showed up at the library and printed two copies of her manuscript. She'd gone to the store beforehand to pick up two giant clips—she wasn't about to have a repeat of the bakery incident. At least this time, if she dropped one of the manuscripts, the pages would stay together.

"This is for you," she told Dylan, putting one copy on the library desk in front of her friend.

Dylan picked it up, reading the title with Evvie's name and email address underneath. "Ev," she said, "is this your manuscript?"

Evvie nodded, a self-satisfied grin on her face. She imagined her happiness like rays of light shining out of her body; she couldn't keep it contained, and she didn't want to. She wanted everyone to know how good she was feeling.

"You . . . you want me to read it?" Dylan held the papers like they were made of the most fragile glass, like they were the most valuable thing she'd ever held.

"I do. It still isn't finished, but maybe your feedback can help me get there. And I want your *honest* feedback, warts and all. Don't hold back. If I'm going to make this story really good, I need to know what's wrong with it."

Dylan nodded slowly. "Thank you. Truly, I'm honored. I'm

going to put this in my office, and I'll start reading it after work. Congratulations, by the way." She came around the desk and hugged Evvie, the movement so genuine and forward for Dylan that tears sprang to Evvie's eyes.

"Thank you. But for what?"

"For trusting me with this." Dylan squeezed her so hard, the breath left her lungs. "I know how much this book means to you."

When Dylan let go, she looked at Evvie with pride, and Evvie had to turn away to avoid dissolving into a blubbering mess.

She sat in the library and knitted for a while, listening to a podcast about the newest romance releases. Then she, Dylan, and Frankie met Minnie at the diner for lunch.

"Thanks again for helping me with this," Minnie said after they'd talked through the proposal plans. Everything was booked and ready to go. "I wish I wasn't so prepared, to be frank. The more I wait, the more difficult it is to keep this from Eleanor. Every time I see her at home, I have to stop myself from popping the question right then and there."

Evvie grabbed Minnie's hand and gave it a squeeze. The two of them hadn't been close friends for long, but they'd bonded quickly. It was interesting how you could live in the same small town with someone for decades and not truly know them. Everywhere Evvie looked, she was reminded that relationships took effort.

"Trust me, I know how difficult it is to keep secrets," she said, thinking of her own that she'd been struggling to keep until after their discussion. "But keeping this one for just a little bit longer will make everything that much better. I can't believe everything you've set up! The solstice is going to be amazing."

"Is it?" Minnie looked so lost, so unsure of herself.

"It is, you'll see," Frankie said. "Trust yourself, too."

Dylan added, "You're a strong, capable woman. You opened your own damn shop! You essentially ran the Sunflower Festival for years. This is nothing."

Minnie crossed her arms. "It sure doesn't feel like nothing."

"Well, it's not *nothing*," Evvie said. "It's a pretty big *something*, but it's going to go off without a hitch. You've got us three to help you." Dylan and Frankie nodded in agreement.

Minnie smiled but didn't say anything, and Evvie couldn't keep her news quiet any longer.

"Not to detract from your plans, Minnie, because they are spectacular . . . but I have news of my own I need to share before I explode into rainbow confetti."

Dylan narrowed her eyes at Evvie. "Something seemed up with you, but I thought maybe it was the thing you gave me earlier. It's not, is it?" Evvie appreciated how Dylan kept her story under wraps, even now.

"Nope," she said, popping the *p*. "It's even better." She inhaled and held her breath, looking at the wonderfully expectant expressions of her friends. "You know Matthias? The man I've been helping lately with his writing project?"

"How could we forget?" Frankie asked with a wry look at Dylan.

"I have been informed, yes," Minnie said. She clearly wasn't as enamored with Iridium Twilight as Dylan was.

Evvie nodded. "He came with me to the queer seniors' meeting last night, and when I dropped him off at his house, right as it began to snow, he asked me to be his partner!" It sounded like a fairy tale, like a Hallmark movie, like the perfect love story to tell on a cold winter's night.

Frankie squealed, Minnie beamed at her, and Dylan shook her head, her expression somewhere between a smirk and a grin. "Look at you," she said. "You're on a roll, my friend."

"Give us details," Frankie said, leaning forward and resting her chin on her fists. "How did he ask you? Did he kiss you?"

Evvie told them the whole story, her joy matching the feeling of wearing a big poofy dress and spinning in circles so the skirt puffed up. "He's coming to my house on Saturday for dinner, and so we can work on his project more. I think we're almost finished with it, actually."

"So you have more time to *get it on*," Dylan said, waggling her eyebrows.

Evvie gasped and pretended to be taken aback. "That is not my intention. But if we do any canoodling, it will be a nice bonus."

Minnie covered her ears. "I do not need to hear about this."

Dylan snickered, and Frankie nudged her.

They chatted for a few more minutes about Matthias—Evvie told them about the market and looking for a Christmas tree—then they dispersed. Minnie and Dylan went back to their jobs, Frankie to walk the dogs, and Evvie to her house to bask in her happiness.

CHAPTER TWENTY-TWO

MATTHIAS

*W*hen Matthias entered the living room on Wednesday morning, Sophie stared out the front window, bouncing on her toes. She wore white footie pajamas patterned with reindeer. "Opa," she said. "Can we build a snowman?"

Matthias went over to see what had put that idea in her mind. Their front yard was a winter wonderland. It had snowed lightly throughout the previous afternoon, but overnight it must have gotten heavier, and now there was a good foot of it on the ground. It weighed down the tree branches, lined the fence rails, and made their cars into giant white blobs.

"That's a fantastic idea," he said. "And we could invite someone else over who would *love* to build a snowman with us."

As he expected, Evvie responded to his invitation text with an enthusiastic "Yes, please!"

Etta had been up early but everyone else had gotten up late, so Matthias and Nick made pancakes—with Sophie's help, of course —and they all enjoyed brunch together with sunlight streaming through the front window and around their newly decorated tree. Many ornaments sparkled in the sun, a few throwing geometric reflections on the floor and walls.

Maybe it was the atmosphere, but everyone seemed to be getting along with Nick now. Sophie liked him, asking him to color with her constantly. And he'd taken an unexpected interest in the chickens, which endeared him to Etta. Matthias wasn't even frustrated with him anymore, not now that Evvie was officially his partner and Nick had stopped rubbing it in that he'd been right.

After breakfast, Bea went to shower, and Etta and Nick took Sophie outside to see the chickens, leaving Matthias to clean the kitchen. He didn't mind. It gave him a chance to gather his thoughts. More accurately, to think about Evvie.

They'd been apart for less than forty-eight hours, and he missed her.

Evvie said she'd be there around one, so Matthias expected her to show up at one-thirty or later. He'd learned long ago with Nick that if someone was chronically late, it was better to expect them late and avoid disappointment. But at a quarter after, there was a knock at the door.

"You're early," he said, opening the door to see her fully ready for a day in the snow. She looked adorable in her navy snow pants, pink puffy coat, white snow boots, bright blue mitts, rainbow scarf, and fluffy lilac earmuffs.

"I'm not, am I?" she said. "I told you one, and isn't it after one?"

He laughed. "Yes, you did. You're right on time."

Looking satisfied, she stepped into the house and stood on her toes to kiss him. Her lips were pleasantly cool. She was carrying a Yellow Brick Books tote bag, which she leaned against the wall. It made a distinct *thunk*.

"What's in there?" he asked.

She waved a mittened hand. "You'll see. Should I take all this winter gear off, or are we going outside right away?"

Just then, Sophie ran into the room wearing pink snow pants and a penguin hat. She skidded to a stop and looked at Evvie. "We match!" she cried, leaning down comically to look at her pants, which were just a shade off from Evvie's jacket.

"We do!" Evvie clapped.

"We don't," Nick said as he came in the back door, grinning. "Hello, Matthias's *real* girlfriend."

Evvie rolled her eyes. "Hi, Nick."

"I guess we're going outside right away," Matthias said. "Nick, wear my extra coat if you're coming with us."

He had no doubt Evvie would fit in with his family. She was already friends with Etta, she'd bonded with Sophie immediately, and Bea would like her for sure once she spent more time with her. Nick was the only wild card, but Evvie could handle her own.

What he was nervous about was how *he* would fit in with them all. Mixing the band with family always made him nervous; he felt like he was a different person with each group separately, and when they came together, he didn't know how to act.

As he put on his jacket, he resolved to enjoy the present and push all those negative thoughts aside. He couldn't be there for the people he cared about if he was stuck inside his head.

Once Sophie was fully bundled up, she ran out into the snow, throwing herself onto her back and making a snow angel.

"Oh, that looks fun!" Evvie said, rushing after her. She lowered herself into the snow, and Matthias laughed at the two of them swishing their arms and legs through it. Nick joined them shortly after, still in his jeans.

Bea came up beside Matthias, putting on her own jacket. "Can you take a picture of this?" he asked her. "I'm terrible with cameras."

"On it," Bea said, whipping out her phone. She snapped a few photos then turned to Matthias. "I like her," she said, leaning against his arm.

"You do?" He gave her a surprised, yet pleased, look. Bea had barely interacted with Evvie yet.

"I do. She makes you happy. And Sophie likes her."

He couldn't argue with that.

"Can I get a little help up, please?" Nick asked, the only one still lying in the snow. Bea rolled her eyes and went to give him a hand. Matthias shook his head fondly; Nick needed a reminder sometimes that he wasn't as spry as he used to be.

The cold made Matthias's knee stiff and sore, so he hung back and watched his girls—all four of them—plus Nick, build a snowman. Etta insisted the snowman needed an animal companion, so they formed a snow chicken at its feet.

"It has no face," Sophie said, frowning at the snowman. "Opa, can we make a face?"

"Of course, baby." Matthias went inside, scrounging around in the fridge and the cupboard. A few minutes later, he headed back out with a basket holding a carrot, a bag of chocolate chips, and a box of Oreos. "Will these work?"

"Yes!" Sophie yelled, diving for the Oreos.

Bea swooped in and took the box. "Okay, honey, those are for the snowman, right? Not for you to eat."

Sophie pouted but acquiesced. It didn't stop her from sneaking a cookie when her mother wasn't looking, though. Nick may have helped with that, and Matthias didn't stop him.

The snowman and the snow chicken soon had faces, and Etta and Sophie found sticks for the snowman's arms.

"It's almost perfect," Evvie said, looking at the snowman with her head tilted as if she were an art critic. "What do you think it's missing, Soph?"

Sophie stood beside Evvie and mimicked her stance, right down to the head tilt. "Hmm. A hat?" Sophie went to pull off her own hat, but Bea admonished her, saying she'd catch a cold.

"Let's use mine." Etta pulled off her purple knitted toque. It was a bit small for the snowman's head, but it worked.

"He needs a scarf too, I think," Evvie said, unwinding her rainbow one. She draped it around the snowman's neck. "There we go. What do you think?"

"B-E-A-U-tiful!" Sophie said, clapping in delight.

Bea insisted they take photos with the snowman. "I can take them." Nick held out his hand, and Bea gave him her phone. They took a couple nice pictures then a few goofy ones.

Matthias looked at all their cold-flushed faces, his heart full. *This* is what he'd always wanted. His family, together and happy. His best friend having wholesome fun with them. The thought of his other kids shot a pang of guilt through his chest, but he couldn't have everything.

Being here with Bea and Sophie, with Etta, with Evvie, even with Nick . . . that was enough. It was *more* than enough. It was a feast for his soul, and he loved every minute of it.

"Why don't I make us some hot chocolate?" he asked as Etta came to stand beside him, looking happy but tired.

"I'll help you," she said. "I need a breather."

Bea joined them. "Me too. I need to fix my hair, anyway." She hadn't worn a hat, and her hair was frizzing out of its bun. "Sophie, you ready to come inside?"

"No, Mama. I want to play more," Sophie whined.

Evvie was sitting on the ground with her, the two of them building a snow structure of some sort. "I can stay with her," she offered.

Bea shrugged. "Alright. Don't stay out too long, though, you two troublemakers."

Evvie winked at Matthias, and he grinned.

"I'll holler when the cocoa is ready," Etta said, heading inside.

"I'd stay out too, but I see now why snow pants are important." Nick patted his jeans, which were now frozen stiff. "I have regrets." He was clearly struggling to bend his knees, wincing every time he moved.

"Stiff knees?" Matthias asked.

Nick nodded and winced again.

"Dry clothes and hot water should do the trick." Matthias threw an arm around his friend's shoulder and led him inside, leaving the sounds of laughter behind them.

CHAPTER TWENTY-THREE

EVVIE

*E*vvie and Sophie built a little snow castle together, and they populated it with all sorts of mythical beings: elves, dragons, unicorns, and even mermaids who lived in the moat around the snowy walls.

As much as Evvie loved playing in the snow, she was relieved when Loretta called them in for hot chocolate. She'd had to pee for at least half an hour, but she hadn't wanted to take off all her snow gear, and she couldn't leave Sophie outside by herself.

Once inside, she stripped off as fast as she could and went to relieve herself, grateful that Matthias had offered to hang up her wet snow clothes in the mud room.

She joined everyone else in the kitchen around the table for hot chocolate and Oreos. Once they'd had their fill, Bea put *The Grinch* on the TV, and she and Sophie cuddled on the couch together as they watched. Loretta wrapped herself in a blanket and joined them, while Nick went to take a bath to warm up. Matthias and Evvie stayed sitting at the table together.

Evvie scooted her chair as close to his as it could go. "That was fun," she said quietly. "Thank you for inviting me."

His smile made her heart flutter. "Thank you for coming, and for being so good with Sophie."

"She's a good kid."

"She really is. And you seem to get along with Bea too. And Nick."

"Nick really isn't that bad, once you get to know him. Unpredictable, maybe, but I see why you like him." Evvie held out her hand, interlacing her fingers with his. Her hands were still cold. His were warm, and worn from his years of playing drums. She couldn't help but imagine how they'd feel on her body, the way he could use his fingers . . . She blinked hard, glad no one could see the thoughts behind her eyes. "And I like Bea," she said, forcing herself to focus on the conversation. "I hope she likes me too."

"You took Sophie off her hands for a good hour, so I'm sure she likes you," Matthias whispered playfully.

As Evvie laughed, she started to shield her mouth with her hand but thought better of it, letting her teeth show.

They were quiet for a minute, listening to the Whos on TV sing about Christmas.

Evvie glanced at her tote bag, still leaning against the wall. Now was as good a time as any to give him her manuscript. She pulled her hand out of his, making him frown. "I have something for you."

As quietly as she could, she went and got her bag, bringing it back to the table.

"Do you want to go to my room?" he asked.

"Sure." She followed him down the hall and into a room that smelled like pine and a light smokiness, like him. Two suitcases were open on the floor. The clothes in one of them were neatly folded—sweaters and shirts stacked in one pile, jeans in another. Rumpled T-shirts and a pair of ripped jeans spilled out of the other one. Evvie would bet her collector's edition of *The Wizard of Oz* on which suitcase was Matthias's and which was Nick's.

"It's a bit messy," Matthias said. "Nick's sleeping on the couch, but one of these is his. You get used to living out of a suitcase, and then putting your clothes in drawers or hanging them up seems like too much effort."

"I don't mind." She sat on his bed, which creaked slightly, and he eased himself down beside her, wincing a bit and straightening his left leg. "Your knee?"

"It's the cold," he said. "I've got screws in there, and they don't react well to cold temperatures. Even when it rains, my knee aches."

"Sorry," she replied, wishing she could take away his pain.

He shrugged. "So you have something for me?"

"Yes." Before she pulled out the manuscript, she turned to face him directly. "I thought about what you said, about putting pressure on myself with my writing. You were right. I'm never going to become better if I never show other people my work. I can't cling to my darlings, because my darlings might be ugly and I don't even know it."

He laughed. "That's one way to put it."

Twisting the bag's handles between her hands, she continued, "I gave a copy of my manuscript to Dylan. She's only read a bit so far, but her feedback has been encouraging. And I want to learn; I want to get better." Taking a deep breath, she pulled the manuscript out. "I printed this off for you yesterday, and that's my email on the front so you can send me your thoughts. I know you're not a big romance novel reader, but I trust you. And I'm starting small. There are a few chapters missing from the end still."

As she handed him the stack of papers, his expression sobered. He looked from her to the manuscript, his eyebrows raised as if questioning that she was truly giving it to him. She nodded, and he held the story much like Dylan had.

"You're sure about this?" he asked, his voice hushed.

"Yes. You've been so vulnerable with me, so . . . this is me being vulnerable with you."

"Evvie." The way he said her name made her feel like she could float on a cloud. "Thank you. I look forward to reading this." He put the manuscript on his night table, lining up the pages just-so with the edge of the wood.

He settled beside her again and lifted a hand, cupping the nape of her neck. "Thank you," he repeated, leaning in to kiss her softly, slowly.

After a few seconds, she giggled.

"What?" he asked, pulling back.

"Sorry, it's just . . . we're kissing in here while your sister, daughter, and granddaughter are out there watching *The Grinch*. And Nick is in the bath across the hall. It feels a bit like we're hiding. Or doing something forbidden."

"Ah, yes. We even closed the door, which is always against the rules. Who knows what we could be doing in here?" There was fire in his eyes, and suddenly he was tickling her.

She shrieked and slapped her hand over her mouth, then they both dissolved into giggles.

A moment later, there was a knock at the bedroom door. "Dad? Evvie? Is . . . is everything alright?"

Evvie snorted and went to open the door. "Just fine, thank you, Bea," she said. "Your father is a villain, that's all."

Bea nodded, her lips pressed together. "I'm not sure I want to know what that means. But I'm glad everything is okay." With that, she backed away slowly then returned to the living room.

Evvie shut the door, and she and Matthias burst out laughing once again.

ALL DAY ON SATURDAY, Evvie fretted about what to make Matthias for dinner. She knew he liked hot chocolate and popcorn, but they hadn't had an actual meal together. She vaguely recalled that Loretta was vegetarian, but was Matthias? Texting him to ask would have been the easy solution, but Evvie felt like she should *know*. A good partner would be able to figure it out, wouldn't they?

And she was determined to be a good partner to Matthias. She hadn't dated in decades, not enough to have a real relationship. But her marriage had ended in a flaming pile of crap, and she hadn't seen it coming, so she had to be alert and intentional this time. Which is why she'd opted to not have any wine that evening; she could take her medication and stay focused.

Dessert was something she could take care of easily, at least. She made Nanaimo bars, which were a breeze to put together. They were a Canadian classic, and if Matthias didn't like them, she'd question his character.

Only forty minutes before Matthias was set to come over, she ran to Juniper Foods and picked up pasta noodles and cheese. Baked macaroni and cheese was one of her comfort foods, the breadcrumbs and extra cheese on top perfectly crisp and tasty. She often added bacon, but she left it out this time just in case.

The doorbell rang as she was combining the noodles and cheese. She hadn't set the table yet, but that was alright. She adjusted her braid, smoothed her pink sweater, took a breath, and opened the door.

"Good evening," she said. Matthias was wearing a navy sweater with elbow patches, which made him look like a tenured professor. His style wasn't what she'd expected from the drummer of a rock band, but it fit his demure personality. Nick was the one with the loud graphic T-shirts, and they suited him.

Matthias leaned in to kiss her before she could say another word.

"Mm," she said against his lips. "I could get used to this."

He laughed, and she mirrored him, one hand over her mouth as she gestured him inside.

"Why do you do that?" he asked.

"Do what?"

"Cover your mouth when you laugh."

"Oh." She looked at her hand. "I'm not sure." Now overly aware of her mouth, she kept her lips pressed firmly shut while she thought, but nothing came to mind. "I can't think of a reason."

The topic faded into unimportance as they moved into the kitchen. Matthias didn't seem to mind that the food wasn't quite ready yet. He made himself comfortable at the table and told her about the one-person play Sophie had put on that morning.

Dinner went well, and Evvie broke down and asked him his favorite foods so she could make them for him. "I can cook too, you know," he said. "Just because I spent most of my life on the road doesn't mean I eat instant noodles every day."

"I know. I just enjoy making things for the people I love." Evvie realized what she'd said and gathered their plates, making as much noise as she could while doing so. "I made Nanaimo bars for dessert." She avoided his gaze. "If you like those."

"I do," he said, a laugh in his voice. She ignored him and carried the plates to the sink.

He finished clearing off the table while she filled the sink, then she asked him to put the coffee on while she washed dishes. They worked together well, moving through the space like they often made dinner and cleaned up as a couple.

She was washing the cutlery, her sleeves pushed up around her elbows, when he came up behind her, wrapping an arm around her shoulders. There was something immensely satisfying about his height in comparison to hers. He was tall enough that she could lean her head back against his chest, right under his chin.

He was warm against her back. "Thank you for making dinner." He leaned down to brush his lips against the side of her neck. Her breath came quicker, and as he drew a line with his nose up to her ear, she shivered, need pulsing between her legs. Good gravy, canoodling was definitely on the menu.

"Did you want to finish your story tonight?" she asked breathlessly.

"Mm, probably," he said, and she gasped as he took her earlobe into his mouth, nipping lightly. She had an impressive collection of vibrators in her night table drawer, but none of them made her feel like this.

The coffee finished brewing and Matthias went to pour himself a cup, leaving Evvie aching. It was cruel of him to do that to her, and she loved it.

"Want a cup?" he asked, his tone completely different than it'd been thirty seconds before. He knew exactly what he was doing, she was sure of it, and she wouldn't give him the satisfaction of seeing her squirm.

"No, thank you. I'll have tea." Ignoring him, she made herself a cup of lemon ginger tea.

They settled in the living room on either side of the couch, her feet on his lap. Her soles tingled even though he wasn't doing anything but sitting there, looking at her. She licked her lips, pleased when his gaze followed her tongue.

He growled slightly and took out his phone, opening the recording app. "Let's get this over with."

She suppressed a giggle and sipped her tea.

It took a few minutes for Matthias to get into the flow of his story, likely because neither of their minds were on it. Eventually, though, the words came more easily. He skipped large chunks of time before the farewell tour, mentioning the albums they made briefly and covering significant tour stops with a sentence or two. "Nothing interesting happened then," he said. "Everything blurred together after a while, and I think we could all feel when it was time to stop. Our tours had gotten shorter, and Nick was the only one interested in interviews anymore. Steven was tired, I was tired. My knee hurt all the time. We agreed to go on the road one last time, and that was it." He shrugged.

"That's it?" There had to be more to the ending. "Were you sad for it to be over?"

Matthias scratched his jaw. "Sure, sure. The band was my whole life, and setting something like that aside is never easy. But I could see the rest of my life stretching out in front of me . . . whatever's left of it. And I didn't want to spend it on stage. When Bea called to tell me she was concerned about Etta, that was that. I knew where I was needed and what I wanted to do."

He'd put his hands on Evvie's shins some time ago, and now he rubbed them absentmindedly. "I mostly left this out of the story, but . . . I think I told you that Bea isn't my only child."

Evvie nodded, feeling like she was on the precipice of truly knowing Matthias. "You said you had three other kids. Your oldest is Sarah, right?"

"Yeah, yeah, Sarah is my oldest. Bea's the youngest. I'm still friends with her mother, Hannah—she's the only one who wanted to make it work, who was okay with me being gone most of the time. She was fine with me flying her and Bea to visit me, to see shows, to come with me on the road sometimes. I'm thankful for that."

Evvie kept quiet, entranced by the soft expression on Matthias's face and the cadence of his words. They were full of yearning, longing, nostalgia.

"My other two kids, Keira and Hayden . . . I barely know them, just like I barely know Sarah. I can't even call them kids anymore, really; they're grown and have families of their own. With Sarah . . . Amy, her mother, asked me to stay away. She didn't want Sarah to be part of the rock 'n' roll life, she said. I honored that, though it damn near killed me. Keira and Hayden's mom, Madison . . ." He swallowed hard, his jaw clenched. After a minute, he continued, "I tried harder with them. I tried to visit, tried to be around. I wanted to be a good father for them. The distance kept growing, though. I spent so much time on tour, at the studio, at awards shows, at parties. I wasn't there for them like I should have been, and Madi eventually told me she couldn't do it. She could see the . . . the pain I was causing them." He was almost whispering now, his voice trembling.

Evvie swung her legs to the floor and moved to sit beside him, grasping his hands. When he looked at her, his eyes were shining with tears.

"Bea was my saving grace," he said, sniffing. "And now, with Etta . . . I feel like this is my chance to be better. To show them I'm good enough. To show *myself* that I'm good enough."

Evvie's heart went out to him, and she wiped away tears of her own. "You are, Matthias. You are good enough."

CHAPTER TWENTY-FOUR

MATTHIAS

The evening had taken a turn he hadn't expected, but it wasn't terrible. Dinner had been lighthearted and fun. And after dinner, Matthias had barely restrained himself from touching Evvie. He could tell she was just as interested in him, and he planned to indulge that desire later. He'd pulled himself together to get the rest of his story out, and somehow, he'd gotten here.

To his kids. To the parts of himself he kept hidden from the world.

He was glad he'd told Evvie, though. Despite her fidgeting and lack of eye contact as he spoke, he knew she was fully invested in whatever he had to say. It was easy to talk to her. She didn't judge, she didn't give unsolicited advice, and she seemed to know exactly what he needed to hear.

The fact that it'd taken only a few meetings with her to tell the tale of the band saddened him, but he took comfort that they were together now. More than friends.

He wanted to tell her so much more about his life, about himself. He wanted her to know the deepest parts of him, not only how he became a drummer and part of an award-winning band. And he wanted to know the deepest parts of her.

She was still grasping his hands. "You are good enough," she repeated, and she kissed him softly. It was so gentle, so genuine. No one had ever kissed him like that.

"Thank you," he said, smiling at her—at this woman who'd crashed into him and made him believe he could be a good enough father, a good enough brother, a good enough partner.

Leaning forward, he stopped the recording on his phone. "What about you?" he asked, his hand on her knee.

"What about me?"

"I've talked so much about myself these past couple of weeks, I feel like I don't know you nearly as well as you know me. Tell me something about you."

She frowned. "I'm not sure what to say. What do you want to know?"

"What do you want to tell me?"

She pursed her lips, her gaze going distant. "We're a lot alike," she said finally. At his questioning look, she continued, "I have often felt like I'm not enough. Not skinny enough, not queer enough, not a good friend or a good wife."

That took him aback. Not just how insecure she was—which you'd never know from the surface—but that she'd been a wife once. "You were married?"

Nodding, she said, "I was, decades ago." The set of her jaw told him the marriage hadn't been a good one.

"Do you want to talk about it?"

She shrugged. "His name was Simon. We grew up together in Edmonton, and we were high school sweethearts. I thought I was going to be with him forever. Clearly, that didn't happen." Her smile was wry.

He shifted to face her. This was the most he'd heard about her past. She'd told him plenty about her friends and her job, but this was something else. Her eyes looked strained, like even recounting what had happened pained her.

"We were together until Christmas when I was thirty-two."

"He left you at Christmas?" He didn't know shit about the guy besides this, but he wanted to pummel him into the ground.

"It gets better," she said. "I thought everything was going well between us. He'd become distant, but that's normal in relationships, isn't it? No matter how close you are to someone, there are times when you drift apart, when you have your own things happening. Then you come back together, you put in the work to stay connected, and everything keeps going.

"I should have seen the writing on the wall, though. I don't know how I missed it. My rose-colored glasses must have been huge and extra rosy, maybe even heart shaped and framed with sequins."

She stared past him, her mind somewhere else.

"I was Christmas shopping. I got him a new BBQ because ours had breathed its last breath that summer, and I'd gone to a specific shop to get his favorite chocolates. He was supposed to be out with a friend, but when I got home, I heard noises. Moans, if you can believe it, coming from our bedroom. My stomach sank, and I should have turned back. But I went to look anyway . . . to see his face between another woman's legs."

Matthias shook his head, his anger expanding in his chest, his fingers tightening on Evvie's knee. He forced himself to ease his grip as she continued.

"I went completely numb. I don't remember walking into the living room, but somehow I got there and collapsed into a chair. Simon ran out a minute later wearing the housecoat I'd gotten him for his birthday. I didn't see the woman leave, but I heard the front door shut."

She paused, looking at the ceiling as tears filled her eyes.

"I asked him why. Why he'd done it. He looked at me with pity, like he felt sorry for me. He said that I might have been happy, but he wasn't. He said, 'This isn't enough for me anymore.' I knew what that meant. *I* wasn't enough for him anymore."

A few tears fell down her cheeks onto her sweater, and he

brushed them away. "I'm so sorry," he said. "Simon was an asshole."

She laughed softly. "The worst part is that I would have let him go if he had just talked to me. I would have been hurt, but I would have understood. These things happen—people's feelings change. But he went behind my back . . . He broke my trust. What he said . . . It plays in my head still, more often than it should." Her gaze snapped to his as if she'd just realized something. "Oh!"

"Oh?"

"You asked why I cover my teeth when I laugh. I've just remembered . . . Simon told me once that I had big teeth. I started covering my mouth when I laughed after that, and I guess I never stopped."

Matthias clenched his jaw. "You deserve so much better than him. Someone who knows how amazing you are and won't let go of you."

"Someone like you?" When she looked at him again, her eyes were dry and want glinted in her blue irises.

"Yes. Someone like me. A man—a *person*—who values every piece of you."

Her lips parted, her gaze softening. "You value every piece of me?"

"Let me show you."

He wrapped one hand around the back of her head, gently pulling her to him. He kissed her like she'd kissed him, gently and with all of himself in the movement. She ran her hands over his beard, slipped a thumb between their lips, traced the shape of his mouth. He groaned, low in the back of his throat.

She made a satisfied noise in response, her eyelids heavy, her gaze flicking between his eyes and mouth. "How would you feel about skipping dessert?"

He moved his hand to her neck, his thumb in the hollow of her throat, and gently pressed her into the couch cushion. "What would we do instead?" he asked, his voice rough.

Her words were breathy. "My room is upstairs."

"Show me."

She bit her lip and grinned, then got up and led him to her room, looking back every so often with that glint still in her eye. He barely felt the need to use his cane, his body moving on autopilot.

Her room fit her perfectly: plants on the bedside tables; all types of art on the walls, one of the prominent paintings an artistic rendering of a vulva; a bright yellow floral quilt. He took it all in at back of his mind, his focus on her. On Evvie. She walked backward as he moved toward her, stopping at the foot of the bed.

She looked at her feet, her cheeks flushed. "I haven't done this in a while."

He leaned his cane against the bed then stepped closer to her, wrapping his arms around her waist. Evvie might have looked different when she was thirty-two, but regardless of how she looked, how could anyone ever want to leave her? She was so soft, and he wanted to feel every inch of her. He wanted to make her feel good.

"I haven't either," he said, kissing along her jaw. Her breaths became shallow and fast. "We can go slow, if you want."

She slid her hands around his back, under his shirt, leaving trails of fire on his skin.

"I would like that," she said, tilting her head back to give him easier access to her neck.

"Slow it is, then."

As she shivered under his touch, moaning softly, he grinned. He'd never been so eager to take his time.

CHAPTER TWENTY-FIVE

EVVIE

*E*vvie wasn't sure if staying the night would be an option for Matthias, but he'd had no problem texting Loretta and Bea to say he wouldn't be coming home. After tiring each other out—thoroughly and blissfully—they'd fallen asleep together, cuddling with her as the big spoon.

Now she was awake, her head on his chest, his arm holding her close. She smiled and listened to his heartbeat under her ear. Thoughts of their conversation the night before flitted through her mind—how Matthias had, in his own way, felt like he wasn't enough. How Simon had rejected her, had made her feel insignificant and small with one simple sentence. How he'd betrayed her trust and made her feel like she couldn't have faith in anyone's love for her again.

After last night, Simon's words didn't hold the same power over her, as if they had faded. In this moment, Evvie felt like she could conquer the world. It was terrifying, but she wanted to trust Matthias with her whole being. She hoped Matthias felt the same.

He stirred, and she propped herself up on one elbow, not wanting to leave the comfort of his embrace. His eyes fluttered open, a smile growing across his face when he saw her. "Good morning," he said, his voice hoarse.

"Good morning," she chirped, leaning forward to kiss him. "How'd you sleep?"

"Like a rock."

"Mm, me too." Her stomach growled. "Ready to face the day?"

He grunted. "Do I have to?"

She ran a hand over his chest lightly, tracing swirls on his skin through his chest hair. "Not yet, if you don't want to. I could bring you breakfast and coffee?"

"Hmm." He closed his eyes, still smiling. "How do you feel about Nanaimo bars for breakfast?"

Her jaw dropped. "Are you serious?"

His eyes snapped open. "Yes? Unless that's a bad idea, then no, I was joking."

She kissed him again. "I didn't know until this moment that you were the perfect man. I would *love* to have Nanaimo bars for breakfast." With that, she got out of bed, humming as she brushed her teeth and went downstairs to get their treats.

As she put the coffee machine on, she glanced out the window. A thin sheet of snow blanketed the ground, sparkling in the morning sun. Evvie squealed and danced in place. Waking up with Matthias, dessert for breakfast, and snow outside . . . she was living her very own fairy tale.

The two of them spent a lazy morning together in bed. At one point, Evvie worked up the courage to ask, "Have you . . . have you had a chance to look at my story yet?"

"I have."

She bit her lip. "And?"

"I'm enjoying it so far. As you said, it's not exactly my genre, but it's well written, and I had no idea I'd be so invested in a book about a baking show."

"Really?" She slouched back and let out a long breath.

"Thank the stars." After a moment, she reached for her tea and gulped it down as if she was in the middle of a desert.

He raised his eyebrows. "You were that worried?"

"Yes, of course! You're only the second person to read it."

"Dylan likes it so far, doesn't she?"

"Yes, but she barely counts. As my best friend, she's obligated to like it."

"And as your partner, I'm not?"

Evvie's eyes widened again. "Son of a motherless goat, Matthias, you can't just say things like that. Now how do I know you're telling the truth?"

He reached for her hand, rubbing his thumb across her knuckles. "My mother always told me not to make promises lightly, not to even say *yes* or *no* unless I truly meant it. I mean this, Evvie. I am saying *yes*, your story is good. I haven't read a ton of it yet, but I like it. I'm excited to read more."

Her shoulders relaxed. "Thank you. That means a lot to me. But make sure to take note of what I can do better, too." The idea of reading people's criticism tied her stomach in knots, but she wouldn't get any better without it.

"I will. I have a notepad with me while I read so I can jot down thoughts."

She beamed at Matthias and was about to ask what point of the story he was at when his phone rang. "It's Bea," he said before he answered.

Evvie went to shower to give him privacy. When she got out, he was fully dressed and the bed was made.

"The girls want to go skating today," he said. "I'd like to go with them, even if I can't be on the ice." His forehead wrinkled as he frowned. "Is that okay?"

Evvie crossed her arms. "Is that *okay*? Geez Louise, Matthias, you don't need my permission to spend time with your family."

He laughed. "I know, that's not what I meant. I guess I just didn't know how you wanted to spend the day. It's been a while since I've had a partner"—Evvie's heart warmed at the word—

"and I'm not sure how we navigate stuff like this. Especially since neither of us currently has a job."

She walked up to him and put a hand on his cheek, savoring the scratchiness of his beard against her skin. "Go spend time with your girls," she said. "I've got dinner tonight with mine, so it's not a problem. Even if I had no plans, it'd be fine."

"If you had no plans, I hope you'd come with me."

"I would. Probably. But I can't today, so have fun without me."

He turned his head to kiss her palm. "Okay, okay. But I want you to come over to my place again soon."

"Deal."

AFTER MATTHIAS LEFT, Evvie spent the rest of the morning and most of the afternoon reading, knitting, and relaxing—recovering from the night before. Her main form of exercise these days was walking, and the things she'd done the previous night had required more of her than she'd remembered. Muscles ached where she didn't even know she had muscles, but it had been more than worth it.

Dylan, Frankie, Minnie, and Eleanor were coming to her house for their weekly Sunday-night dinner, so she tidied the main floor before they arrived. Dylan and Frankie were the first over, and Evvie practically word vomited her update before they had taken off their coats.

"Better than your vibrators, huh?" Dylan smirked.

"I'm happy for you, Evvie," Frankie said, giving her a hug.

When Eleanor and Minnie arrived, Evvie got to tell the story all over again, and it filled her with as much energy as it had the first time.

Everyone was in a good mood throughout dinner. Even Minnie seemed more animated than usual, talking about their plans for Christmas with Vera and Kat, Eleanor's daughter and grandchild. Evvie suspected the upcoming proposal had something to do with Minnie's excitement.

"What are you doing for Christmas, Ev?" Dylan asked. "You don't have a tree yet. I thought you might have picked one out the other day when you went with Matthias and Loretta."

Evvie ducked her head. "I didn't. I wasn't sure . . . I mean, we usually spend Christmas together. But this year"—she looked at Frankie—"I don't want to get in the way."

"Evvie," Frankie said, reaching out to squeeze her arm. "You would never get in the way. I assumed we'd be spending Christmas with you! We should have asked."

"Fuck, I'm sorry." Dylan covered her eyes. "Of course we want to spend Christmas with you. If that's what you want."

A wave of relief washed over Evvie. "Thank you." She wanted to spend Christmas with Dylan, but now she had Matthias too, and he'd already invited her to his family gathering. Although that was before they were dating. Evvie suddenly felt torn. Who did she want to be with on Christmas more?

"I . . . I don't know what's going on anymore, actually," she said, frowning. "This thing with Matthias, it's so new. I feel all of a doodah about the holidays." But the idea of Christmas—and her birthday—without Dylan made her chest tighten. "Why don't we spend Christmas Day together for sure? And I'll get back to you about Christmas Eve." Options were always good.

"Works for me," Dylan said, and Frankie nodded. "I ordered a cake for your birthday already, so it'd be a shame if you weren't there to eat it."

"Ooo." Evvie looked fondly at her friend. "Perfect."

She brought out the leftover Nanaimo bars for dessert, shivering in pleasure as memories of the night before flooded her senses. It was unlikely she'd ever be able to eat them again without thinking about Matthias, about how he made her feel.

And she wasn't at all mad about it.

CHAPTER TWENTY-SIX

MATTHIAS

When Matthias got home on Sunday, the girls were putting on their winter gear and getting ready to skate. But Nick, usually the life of the party, was conspicuously absent.

"Is Nick not coming with us?" Matthias asked.

Etta shrugged. "I asked him earlier, and he said *maybe*." She rolled her eyes, as if this was typical of Nick. Which it was.

"Hmm." Matthias frowned. Nick didn't have much else to do and he loved skating, so what was he up to?

"I think he's in your room," Bea added. "I heard him laughing in there earlier."

Maybe Nick was on a video call. Shrugging, Matthias went to see what his friend was doing. When he opened the door to his room, the first thing he saw was the mess of papers all over the bed. "What the . . ."

Nick was reclining against the headboard, reading a page. He blinked at Matthias in that way people do when they're coming out of a good story.

Matthias's heart started pounding before his mind understood what was happening. His eyes went to his night table, where a cup of coffee sat. Where Evvie's manuscript had been sitting. "Oh fuck." He strode into the room and scanned one of the pages, confirming his fears. "Nick, have you been reading this?"

"Yeah." Nick looked at him, the picture of innocence. "Have you started it yet? It's really good."

Matthias groaned. "You can't read any more of it." As fast as he could, he grabbed the pages and restacked them, although they were no longer in order.

"What are you doing?" Nick protested. "I had a system going!"

"Where's the clip?"

Nick pointed to the other side of the bed, his eyes wide. "What's the deal?"

Matthias snatched the paper from Nick's hand and added it to the stack. He shoved the manuscript into his night table drawer. "You are not to touch that again," he said, well aware he was talking to Nick as if he were a child.

"Matty, what's the big deal? Evvie wrote that, didn't she? She's good. I was thinking, actually, we could send it to our agent—"

"No. Nope. Not a chance." Matthias threw his hands up.

"Why not? She could get a publishing deal with this, make it big."

"Nick." Matthias punched the bed. "Listen to me. Evvie is not ready for that. I'm only the second person who has ever read her writing. She's still working on this story, trying to make it better. It's not even finished. And she cares about who sees it, okay? She did not give you permission to read it."

Nick sipped his coffee, avoiding Matthias's gaze. "Well, yeah, but she's a good writer."

"It doesn't matter." Why was Nick so infuriating sometimes? "Do you remember how precious we were about our first songs? How much we loved those lyrics? How nervous we were to put out our first album?"

"Yeah, but that's different."

"It's not. In fact, she probably put even *more* heart into this. It is staying in this drawer"—he thumped the door for emphasis —"and it's not coming out again. Got it?"

"Yeah, I got it, Jesus." Nick still wasn't making eye contact with him.

Matthias's heart sank, and he breathed out slowly through his nose. "Nick?" He kept his eyes closed so he wouldn't see his friend's reaction.

"Matty."

"You sent it to her already, didn't you?"

"To who?" Of course he had. Matthias could hear the admission in his voice. Nick was trying to play it cool, but there was a reason he was a singer and not an actor.

"To Shelley." Their agent.

"Just the first fifty pages!"

Matthias groaned and opened his eyes.

"I thought I was being nice," Nick said, his hands up in surrender. "I started reading the story after you left yesterday, and I was sold after the first chapter. I scanned the pages onto my phone—did you know there's an app that can do that now? It's so cool." Matthias glared at him. "Anyway, I scanned them and sent them, and I kind of asked Shelley to prioritize reading it because I thought it would be a nice Christmas surprise to help Evvie get it published. I mean, Shelly might not even know anyone who publishes romance. But I thought it was worth a try."

Matthias clenched his fists. Nick was *always* trying to be nice, like when he baked Steven a peanut butter cake for his birthday, forgetting Steven was deathly allergic to peanuts and sending him to the emergency room. "You can't just read people's writing without asking," Matthias said. "Email Shelley and tell her to forget it. At least, for now. Okay?"

"Yeah, sure, okay."

Chances were high that Shelley hadn't read the pages yet. Nick would tell her to put a pause on reading it, and the whole incident would fade into the past until everyone forgot it even happened.

With that out of the way, Matthias relaxed. Evvie would never know that Nick had read her work, and everything was going to be fine.

CHAPTER TWENTY-SEVEN

EVVIE

*E*vvie hadn't made any plans on Monday, thinking she'd stay in her pajamas, maybe make cinnamon buns, and read. She started knitting herself a new rainbow scarf as well, since she'd left hers on the snowman at Matthias's house and planned to leave it there for whoever wanted it.

Just before noon, Eleanor phoned. "Would you like to go for lunch? I know we just saw each other last night, but I thought we could do something different and go to that ramen place."

There was only one ramen restaurant in Juniper Creek, so Evvie knew exactly where Eleanor meant. "Sure. Is everything alright?"

"Yes, everything's wonderful. We haven't gone out just the two of us in a while."

Less than an hour later, they sat in a cozy booth at Main Street Ramen, each with a steaming bowl in front of them. Ramen was a perfect soul-warming food for the cold winter day. They talked about the weather, the holidays, and how Eleanor's shop was doing. Evvie told Eleanor about building a snowman and getting to know Matthias's family. Eleanor had heard of Iridium Twilight but didn't listen to them, so her interest was more in Matthias as a person than as a drummer. Evvie even talked about Nick, about how he wasn't as bad as Evvie had expected. "He's really good with Sophie, and he seems like a good guy, if a bit clueless."

While the conversation wasn't stilted or awkward, Evvie could tell Eleanor had something on her mind. Her responses weren't as thoughtful as usual, and she kept drifting off between topics.

"I know you said everything was alright earlier, but is it really? You seem a bit . . . distracted," Evvie said.

Eleanor sighed. "I am. You know Minnie better than Dylan and Frankie do, I think, so I thought maybe you could help." She stared into her ramen, swirling the noodles around. "She seems . . . off, lately. Moodier than usual. And the other day when she was on the phone, I walked into the room and she ran out like her tail was on fire. When I asked who she was talking to, she waved me off and said it wasn't important."

It must have been a call related to the proposal, but Evvie couldn't tell Eleanor that. And of course she'd noticed Minnie's extra moodiness, but she understood it completely. She couldn't tell Eleanor about the reason behind it.

"Maybe it truly wasn't important," Evvie said, trying to sound nonchalant.

"Then she shouldn't have had a problem telling me who was on the other line." Eleanor slumped in her seat, which was unlike her. "I think she's hiding something from me."

Shiitake mushrooms. Evvie gulped and quickly took a sip of water to hide it. How was she supposed to handle this? She didn't want to lie to Eleanor, but she couldn't tell her the truth without blowing up the whole plan.

"Eleanor . . . you're putting me in a tough spot here."

"I am?" Eleanor furrowed her brows.

Honesty was the best policy, and Evvie couldn't go against it. "Listen. I know something, but I can't tell you what it is. I need you to trust me. Everything is okay with Minnie."

"It is?" Eleanor's entire body seemed to sag with relief. "Nothing bad is happening?"

"Not at all. I think you'll be pleased in the end. But that's all I can tell you." Evvie held her breath, hoping Eleanor wouldn't push for more information. If she did, Evvie didn't know that she could keep the secret.

Luckily, Eleanor seemed satisfied. "Alright. I do trust you, even though this is enormously frustrating."

Evvie wanted to tell her she wouldn't have to be frustrated for much longer—the winter solstice was in three days—but even that felt like revealing too much. "I'm sorry," she said. "I wish I could tell you more. But it's in your best interests that I don't."

Eleanor narrowed her eyes at Evvie, but she smiled. "I suppose I can suffer temporarily for my best interests. Even if the suspense sends me to an early grave."

Evvie grinned. "I sure hope it doesn't."

They finished lunch in good spirits, then Evvie went home while Eleanor headed back to her shop.

Thank Judy Garland Evvie hadn't had to lie. One fake date had been more than enough trust breaking for her.

WHEN EVVIE GOT HOME, she opened her laptop to check her email. While she'd been out for lunch, Dylan had texted her; she'd finished reading another few chapters and sent her feedback. Dylan's verbal encouragement reassured Evvie, but she hadn't had the guts to look at Dylan's suggestions. She'd been flagging all of Dylan's emails to look at them later, once the manuscript was finished and she was ready to revise.

Dylan's email was in her inbox, as expected, but there was another one right above it that set Evvie's heart thumping. It was from someone named Shelley Baker with the subject line "Forwarded Your Manuscript." Blinking rapidly, Evvie opened the email.

Hello Mrs. Adler,

I received your manuscript pages, and they're wonderful! Unfortunately, I don't take on romance clients, so I forwarded your manuscript to an agent friend of mine who will adore *Love Takes the Cake*. You should hear from her in the coming weeks. Her name is Brooklyn Finch.

Happy holidays!
Shelley Baker

Evvie could barely breathe. She tried to convince herself the email was a scam, but only two other people knew the title of Evvie's novel, and there it was, in this email from a stranger. Who the flap was Shelley Baker? And how had this person read pages from her manuscript? How had they gotten her email?

The words "Literary Agent" were in the email signature, and Evvie's eyes kept going back to them. She tried to talk herself out of a panic attack, but she couldn't sit still. She had to do something. Scooching her chair back, she left her computer open on the table and hurried to put on her boots and coat.

Five minutes later, she pounded on Dylan's door. Frankie opened it, Darcy and Bingley—Dylan's dogs—wagging their tails behind her. Frankie was wearing sweats and a hoodie, her feet encased in bunny slippers. Evvie would have commented on those had it been any other day. "Evvie? Are you okay?"

"Where's Dylan?"

"She's in a meeting at the libra—"

Evvie brushed past Frankie, stopping to take her shoes off but keeping her coat on. She halted in the middle of the living room, realizing what Frankie had been saying. "Oh."

Frankie approached Evvie slowly, like she was afraid she'd scare her off. "Why don't you sit down? I'll go get Dylan."

"Alright. Yes, I'll do that." She let Frankie guide her to the couch, where she sat, still wearing her coat. The dogs followed her over and Bingley jumped up beside her, licking her hand. She barely felt it.

"I'll be right back," Frankie said.

Evvie heard the door open and close, but she didn't register much else until Dylan was standing in front of her.

"Evvie?" her best friend said gently. "What's wrong?"

Blinking at Dylan, Evvie took a deep breath. She'd known the answer before she even left her house, but she had to ask. "Did you send my manuscript to someone named Shelley Baker?"

"No . . . Who's Shelley Baker?"

Without answering, Evvie grabbed her phone and opened her mail app, pulling up the email. She shoved the phone at Dylan as Bingley rested her head on Evvie's thigh.

"Oh shit," Dylan said as she skimmed it. "Who the fuck is Shelley Baker?"

Frankie stood in front of them, her arms crossed. "What's going on?"

Dylan grabbed Evvie's hand then looked at Frankie and explained the email. Evvie gripped Dylan's fingers as if they were a lifeline. If she let go, the world would crumble around her.

"Okay, let's think about this," Frankie said. She must have put her slippers back on at some point, or maybe she never took them off. She tapped her toe on the floor, the ears of the fabric bunny flopping up and down. Evvie didn't need to think about it, but she let Frankie talk it out, hoping she'd missed something. "How many people did you show your manuscript to?"

"Only two," Evvie replied, her voice rough. "Just Dylan and . . ." She couldn't say his name.

"Matthias." Dylan bit out the syllables.

Frankie's voice was calm as she asked, "Has Matthias ever mentioned someone named Shelley Baker?"

Evvie shook her head. He hadn't, but he was working on a book. And that book had an agent.

"Hmm. It sounds like you need to talk to him."

"Hey, Ev, can you please loosen up a bit?" Dylan asked, lifting their joined hands.

Evvie was squeezing Dylan's hand so hard, her fingers were turning white. "Holy toboggan sled, I'm sorry." She forced herself to let go, and Dylan winced as she flexed her hand. "I don't think I can talk to him right now. How could he do this?" She stared at Frankie's bunny slippers, but she wasn't truly seeing anything.

"Frankie, can you get Evvie some tea, please?"

Evvie heard Dylan's words as if they came through a tunnel.

"Let's get your coat off, and you can stay here for a while, okay? Have you eaten anything?"

Had she? "Lunch. I went for lunch with Eleanor."

"Okay, good. I'll get you a muffin anyway." Dylan helped Evvie out of her jacket and handed her a blanket. At some point, a cup of tea and a plate with a muffin appeared on the coffee table in front of them.

Matthias knew how much this story meant to Evvie. He knew she hadn't wanted to show it to anyone, that she only gave it to him and Dylan because she trusted them. Maybe she shouldn't have.

She stayed on Dylan's couch for the rest of the day, cuddling with the dogs. Dylan nudged her to eat dinner, but she could only stomach a few bites. Frankie had put on the Hallmark channel, which was playing nonstop Christmas movies. But Evvie could barely pay attention to them. When she did catch bits and pieces of the stories, they reminded her of Matthias and sent her into a spiral of dread.

The last time she'd felt like this had been when Simon had left her. This wasn't the same scenario, of course—she suspected Matthias had good intentions—but it had taken her decades to move past Simon's betrayal and go on another date, and as soon as she opened her heart to someone else . . . he'd gone behind her back.

He'd broken her trust.

CHAPTER TWENTY-EIGHT

MATTHIAS

*M*atthias called Evvie on Monday, but she didn't answer. Maybe she was busy, so he thought nothing of it. But his heart still lifted when his phone rang on Tuesday morning and her photo appeared on the screen.

"Hey," he said, answering it. "I've missed you. I tried to call yesterday, but you must have been busy."

There was no reply, and for a moment he thought the call had been disconnected. Just as he was pulling the phone away from his ear, she said, "Matthias, I need to talk to you. Can you meet me at the gazebo in the park?"

Something was wrong, he could hear it in her voice. And although she hadn't said *we need to talk*, her words were close enough. "Sure," he said, his stomach filling with lead. His mind raced through the last time they had seen each other; she'd made him dinner, they'd finished the memoir, he'd told her about his kids, they'd had sex. It had been fantastic, but she didn't sound happy. "What time?"

"Can you be there in half an hour?"

Nick insisted on going with him, begging to get out of the house. "Fine, but don't come anywhere near the gazebo," Matthias said. Nick had already messed up enough by reading

Evvie's story and sending it to Shelley. Whatever this was, he wanted Nick to stay far away from it. "Drop me off, go find a parking spot, then go shopping or something. And keep your glasses on." Nick hadn't been pictured by the media in Canada with his glasses on yet, so there was a smaller chance of anyone recognizing him with them. Plus, Matthias didn't trust him to drive without them.

Luckily, Nick seemed to pick up on Matthias's mood. "Is everything okay with you and Evvie?" he asked as they drove into town.

"I don't know." Matthias's gut told him everything was *not* okay, but he couldn't figure out what he'd done. He knew what Nick had done, but Evvie couldn't have known about that. No one knew besides him and Nick. The situation was giving him stress hives.

Nick pulled up to the curb by the park, putting on the hazard lights. "Hey," he said, looking at Matthias with a worried *V* between his brows. "I don't know what's going on, but I hope you work it out. She seems like a keeper. Call me when you're done."

Matthias nodded once then got out, pulling his toque down over his ears. He couldn't remember winter ever being so cold when he was growing up. It seemed pretty chilly to have an outdoor heart-to-heart, but maybe Evvie needed the cold. Winter seemed to comfort her.

But why did she need comforting?

She was easy to spot in her bright pink coat as he walked toward the gazebo, snow crunching under his boots and his cane. She turned toward him as he approached, but she didn't wave or even say hello.

He stopped a few feet away, standing in front of where she sat on the bench. "Hi," he said, his breath visible in the cold air.

No reply. She stared at her gloved hands, seeming to struggle with something. As he stood there, keeping a respectful distance, his knee started to ache.

Finally, she looked at him, her cheeks flushed and her eyes glassy. "Who's the agent for your book?"

"What?" That was not what he'd expected her to say, and his heart jumped into his throat.

"For the band's memoir. Who's the agent?"

He tried to keep his expression neutral. "Shelley Baker. Why?"

Her bottom lip trembled, and it killed him to see her like this. Although he didn't know what had made her feel this way, he was starting to get an inkling, and he did not like it. He couldn't take it anymore. Lurching forward, his knee barely holding him, he sat beside her. "Evvie, what's going on? Why are you asking about Shelley Baker?" How had she found out?

She slid away but turned to face him. "Matthias. Did you send her my manuscript?"

He waited a split second too long to answer. "No, of course I didn't."

Something flashed in her eyes. Confusion? Disbelief?

"Please don't lie to me," she said, her tears spilling over.

He reached for her, but she didn't reach back.

She valued honesty, and he couldn't keep the truth from her. He didn't want to—that's not what you did to someone you cared about. "Evvie, I'm not lying. I didn't send Shelley your manuscript. But . . . Nick did."

She huffed out a laugh, a distinctly unamused one, and wiped her nose with her glove. "Of course he did."

Matthias rubbed his hands over his face, his beard and mustache scratching against his gloves. "He only sent the first fifty pages. And he did it because he likes your story! He thinks it's worth publishing."

Evvie shook her head. "Does it matter what he thinks? I trusted *you* with my story, not him."

"I know, I know. But he didn't do it to hurt you. And we emailed Shelley right away to ask her to forget about it. We can trust her."

"It's too late for that. She's already sent it to another agent named Brooklyn Finch." She blinked a few times, her lashes wet with tears. "How long have you known about this?" The anguish in her voice turned his stomach.

"Only since Sunday, I swear. When I got home, Nick was in my room. I had left your manuscript on my night table, and he'd been reading it. But as soon as I saw him, I told him he had no right to do that."

She nodded and wiped her nose again. "Thank you." They sat in silence for a few moments, then she said, "Were you going to tell me about it?"

Matthias wanted to scream. "I thought nothing happen. I made him email Shelley, and I didn't think she'd have read the manuscript yet. Agents are usually super busy."

"So . . . that's a *no*."

"I . . . I didn't think you'd need to know if nothing would come of it."

"But something did come of it."

He didn't know what to say to that, so he said nothing.

For a moment, she looked up at him, her face carefully blank. He thought she might be about to say everything was fine, but instead she stood up and walked out of the gazebo, saying, "I have to go. I'm sorry."

He got up to follow, but there was no way he could catch up to her with his knee in this cold. "Evvie, wait!" he called after her.

She didn't look back.

His hands shaking, Matthias pulled out his phone and dialed Nick's number. "I'm ready."

He didn't look at Nick when he got in the car. He didn't look at him for the entire ride home. And he didn't say a word, no matter how much Nick prodded him.

When they arrived home and got out of the car, Nick said, "Okay, Matty, what did I do?"

Matthias glared at him and slammed the car door. "You know exactly what you did. I want you out of the house."

"What?"

As Nick came around the car, Matthias strode up to him, so close they nearly bumped chests. "You're always sticking your nose in everyone else's business without their permission."

Understanding dawned in Nick's eyes, his wiry eyebrows twitching. "Oh. This is about the manuscript."

"Yeah!" Mattias yelled. "That's what this is about!" He stomped inside, his knee complaining the entire way. He went straight to his room and shoved all of Nick's stuff in his suitcase.

Nick came in a few minutes later, and Matthias pushed the bag at him. "Go," he said. "You wonder why no one answered your calls about Christmas? This is why."

He slammed the door in Nick's face.

Matthias called Evvie later that night, but she didn't answer. He figured she needed space, and he'd honor that. So, he tried to focus on his family and not even think about Nick.

No one had asked about Nick leaving, other than Etta and Bea both asking Matthias if he was okay. They must have heard the shouting. Even Sophie didn't ask, although Matthias suspected that was Bea's doing.

Over the next few days, Etta seemed better than ever, spending more time sketching and baking. Thursday morning, Bea took Sophie to the library for story time, so Etta and Matthias had coffee alone.

"Can I show you something?" Etta asked him, placing her now-empty mug in the sink.

He nodded, and Etta led him out to the barn.

"Do I finally get to know what you've been working on?" he asked. The weather had warmed up in the past two days, not enough to melt the snow, but enough that his knee felt better.

Etta nodded, her eyes twinkling.

When he stepped into the barn, he looked around, expecting to see a project of some kind. But everything was the same—the dirty wooden floor, the musty smell, the cracked wooden boards in the walls. "What am I supposed to see?"

"Nothing yet," Etta said, grabbing her sketchbook from the nearby stool. "Here." She handed it to him.

He leaned on his cane as he opened the book. It took a few pages before he realized what he was looking at. "This is the barn?" The first sketches were rough, some depicting what the barn used to look like when they had cows and horses, back when he and Etta were kids. Then the sketches became more detailed, the building almost unrecognizable. The shape was the same, but the lines were cleaner, sleeker. Then the sketches turned into full scenes, the barn packed with tables and chairs, light fixtures hanging from the ceiling, people eating and dancing.

"What do you think?" Etta asked, looking at him eagerly.

"I think these are good sketches. But what do they mean?"

She gestured at the space around them. "This is what I want to do with the barn."

"Turn it into an events center?"

"Sort of. I want to clean it up and use it as a wedding venue. It's big enough, and rustic weddings are popular right now. In the summer and fall, this area is gorgeous. Can you picture the wedding photos people could get here?"

He could see it, the picture Etta was painting. The barn, fixed up and painted, lighting installed, furniture set up, people mingling. Wedding parties taking photos in the field and against the backdrop of the barn doors. "It's a good idea," he said, impressed. He handed her the sketchbook, and she hugged it to her chest, looking around at the barn as if it was everything she'd ever wanted.

"Are you planning to fix it up yourself?" he asked. "I can help, but I don't know how much I'll be able to do." His energy wasn't what it used to be, and neither was his knee.

"I haven't thought that far," she said. "It might be better to hire people. I have enough saved up, I think. And we'd make a fair amount back from renting out the place."

She continued laying out her ideas as they went back to the house, and her enthusiasm was contagious. By the time she'd talked herself out and gone to her room for a nap, Matthias felt better than he had in days. Her vision was hopeful. Bright.

It made him think of Evvie. She'd love Etta's idea.

Before he could reconsider, he pulled out his phone and called her. He didn't expect her to answer, so when she did, he froze up.

"Matthias? Are you there?" she asked.

"Evvie." Her name was a sigh on his lips. "Sorry, I . . . I didn't think you'd pick up."

"Neither did I, to be honest."

Now that they were talking, he had no idea what to say. Did he beg for her forgiveness? Tell her he missed her? Ask to see her again?

He settled on "I'm glad you answered."

"Matthias . . ."

His chest tightened at her tone, and he knew what was coming.

She continued, "I'm sorry but . . . I don't think I can see you anymore."

He doubled over as if he'd been punched. Even with those few moments of preparation, hearing that was too much. "Why?" He wasn't the one who sent her manuscript to the agent. Why should he be punished for it?

"You're a wonderful man, you truly are. But this whole thing . . . I can't do it right now. I appreciate how you stood up to Nick, but you didn't tell me what he'd done. You weren't going to tell me unless you absolutely had to. I can't be with someone who keeps things like that from me. I'm sorry."

"Evvie—"

"Don't try to talk me out of it, please. This is what I need."

What could he say to that? If this was what she needed, of course he would give it to her. No matter how much it hurt. "Okay," he said, his voice almost a whisper.

"I'm sorry. Merry Christmas."

CHAPTER TWENTY-NINE

EVVIE

*W*hy did he have to call that day, of all days? Evvie had to leave in less than an hour to prepare for Minnie's proposal.

She'd already decided to officially end things with Matthias before Christmas, but now she had to go straight from a break-up to watching her friend propose to her other friend. It's not that Matthias was a bad person; in fact, he was the complete opposite, which made it worse. Evvie wanted to be with him, but this whole thing with her manuscript . . . She'd put herself out there again, and she'd gotten so comfortable. She'd trusted Matthias with a piece of her soul. Nick may have been the one to send it in, but Matthias had known, and he hadn't told Evvie about it. He'd kept it from her, had even played ignorant when she'd first broached the topic at the gazebo. To make matters worse, he'd defended Nick, as if sending in only the first fifty pages made everything not as bad.

If he hadn't been involved at all, things would have been different. But he'd reminded her what it felt like to put yourself in someone else's hands and have them drop you.

Heartbreak seemed inevitable for her.

Dylan and Frankie would be at the proposal, and there was no way Dylan wouldn't notice something was off with Evvie—something even more than before—but she didn't want to talk about it.

Time for the best acting performance of her life.

She drove to the library where Dylan and Frankie were waiting, turning on strings of fairy lights and putting them into mason jars. It was only quarter to four in the afternoon, but the sun was going to set at quarter after, and everything had to be timed exactly right.

"We're almost done with these," Dylan said. "Can you watch for when Minnie and Eleanor leave?"

Nodding, Evvie stood at her post by the window. Ten minutes later, Minnie and Eleanor came into view across the street, stopping by a bench. They would have come from the first event of the proposal: decorating a yule tree at Minnie's.

They were holding hands, Eleanor looking puzzled but happy. Five minutes after that—right on time—a white horse-drawn carriage pulled up in front of them. Evvie couldn't see Eleanor's face, but she could imagine the joy shining in her eyes.

Evvie's eyes filled with tears, and she couldn't tell if they were happy or mournful.

As the women got into the carriage, Evvie called over her shoulder, "They're off." Her voice was little more than a croak, so she had to repeat herself.

"Let's get going," Frankie said, picking up a crate of their homemade lanterns. Dylan grabbed one as well, and Evvie took the last one. The three of them hurried across the street to the bench where Minnie and Eleanor would be dropped off again in ten to fifteen minutes. Which meant Evvie, Frankie, and Dylan had only ten minutes to set up.

"I'll start by the bridge." Frankie made her way through the field. The weather had warmed up today, so the snow slushed against her boots.

Evvie and Dylan set their crates on the bench and began pulling out the lanterns, laying them out to build a path across the field that Minnie and Eleanor would follow to the bridge. To keep from breaking down completely, Evvie tried to focus on the task before her.

As she went back to the bench to grab another armful of jars, a voice said, "Evvie?"

She paused and looked up, stifling a groan. "Nick? What are you doing here?" He was the last person she wanted to see.

"That's the question of the hour, isn't it?" He wore ripped jeans and what looked to be a new winter coat. When she didn't laugh, he grimaced. "Can I talk to you for a minute?"

"I'm kind of busy," she said through gritted teeth. She didn't know how much time was left until Minnie and Eleanor returned, and her half of the pathway wasn't done.

"Please?" Nick said. "It's important."

Dylan appeared from the path, her eyes growing bright and wide. "Nick Evans?" When she glanced at Evvie, her features turned stern. She put her hands on her hips. "Oh, fuck no. I don't care who you are. You're a shit human being, you know that?"

That was going a bit far, but Evvie appreciated Dylan's enthusiasm, especially since Nick was the lead singer of one of her favorite groups.

"I know." Nick kicked at a piece of ice. "That's why I'm here. I want to apologize."

Dylan was about to say something else, but Evvie held up a hand. "If you want to apologize, you'll help us while you're at it. Grab a crate."

He did as she ordered and followed her and Dylan to the unfinished path. Dylan kept glancing at Nick, and Evvie could imagine how much excitement she was suppressing.

"Walk and talk, friend," Evvie said, not looking at Nick as she pulled jars from the crate.

"Ah, right. I'm sorry, Evvie. Matthias told me not to read your story—not to touch it, actually—but it was kinda too late by that point. Honestly, I thought I was doing you a favor."

Evvie scoffed and shook her head as she placed a jar on the ground. Only a few left now, and time was ticking.

Nick continued, "I know now that I was wrong. I broke Matthias's trust and yours, and I feel terrible. He kicked me out of the house for it, and I don't blame him. Just . . . don't take this out on him, okay? It's not his fault. We just met, and I don't know you that well, and I haven't seen you with him all that much, but I can tell you make him happy. He wouldn't have kicked me out for just anybody. And I could tell he was heartbroken in the car the other day after you two talked. So . . . blame me. Not him."

Straightening, Evvie sighed. "It's too late, Nick." She lowered her voice. "I broke up with him this afternoon."

"You what?" Dylan said, having finished connecting their path to the one Frankie had started.

Nick tipped his head back and groaned at the sky. He looked at Evvie with desperation in his eyes. "Can't you take it back? Tell him you want to get back together?"

Tears pressed at the backs of Evvie's eyes. "I can't, Nick. Now, if you'll excuse us, we have a proposal to get to." She swept past him, grabbing the crate as she went. She picked up the other empty crate from the bench then went to meet Dylan. Nick was gone.

"You broke up with Matthias?" Dylan asked.

"This isn't the time," Evvie said, bottling up her emotions like she'd never done before. "They're going to be here any minute."

Dylan looked like she wanted to say more, but she kept quiet, grabbing a crate from Evvie. The two of them met Frankie at the bridge, where she and Kat, Eleanor's grandchild, were putting the finishing touches on a gorgeous archway strung with fairy lights, crystals, and white flowers.

"I'm so excited, I think I'm going to puke," Kat said, stepping back to look at the arch. "You have no idea how hard it was to keep quiet all week. Gran didn't prod, but I could tell she knew something was up."

"You did well, kid." Dylan patted Kat's shoulder.

"Time to hide," Frankie said, ushering them all behind the trees to the side of the bridge. Kat squealed, and Evvie would have done the same if she didn't feel like puking for entirely different reasons.

Waiting in the fading light, trying to stay hidden, was agony. Frankie adjusted her camera, and every click and whir seemed exceedingly loud.

Finally, Minnie and Eleanor's voices floated through the air, growing louder as they approached.

". . . beautiful," Eleanor was saying. "What is all of this?"

"You'll see," Minnie replied.

Evvie couldn't see them walking up, but she knew the moment Eleanor spotted the archway because she gasped. Minnie needed to pop the question sooner than later; the light was fading fast, and Frankie wouldn't be able to get any good photos once the sun dipped below the trees.

Minnie pulled Eleanor in front of the archway, and Frankie snuck into position. Evvie tried not to move, and Dylan gripped her hand. Kat practically vibrated beside them.

"Eleanor," Minnie said, holding Eleanor's hands. "Our relationship may have started in a rocky place, but I am overjoyed to be with you now. You make me a better woman and a better florist. You bring magic to my days and light to my life, and I want to be with you for the rest of it." She pulled a blue box out of her jacket pocket and gently worked off Eleanor's gloves. Tears ran down Eleanor's cheeks, but she was radiant. "Will you do me the honor of becoming my wife?"

Eleanor sniffled. "Yes, of course!"

Minnie slid the ring onto Eleanor's finger, and Eleanor flung her arms around Minnie's shoulders, pulling her in close.

Laughing, Minnie called, "You can all come out now!"

The next few minutes were a blur of hugs and congratulations, and Minnie invited them to her house for a yule log cake and Wassail consumed by candlelight. Vera, Eleanor's daughter, would join them after she got off work at Juniper Foods.

Evvie drove over with Dylan and Frankie, but she felt removed from it all. She was there, but not there. Dylan kept glancing at her, clearly checking in on her. Every time, Evvie shook her head. She did not want to talk about it. She did not want to think about it. She wanted to celebrate Minnie and Eleanor, then go home, curl up in bed, and not come out for days.

They left after an hour or so, giving the newly engaged couple plenty of time to celebrate on their own.

It killed Evvie that she couldn't be as happy for her friends as she wanted to be. She should be over the moon for them, and she was in a way, but seeing their happiness shot daggers into her heart. She could have had that, but she'd lost it.

Happily-ever-afters weren't meant for her.

EVVIE GAVE in to her sadness. She spent the next two days in bed, eating ice cream straight from the tub, making cookie dough to eat instead of bake, and crying through Hallmark movie marathons.

Every time she thought of Matthias, her mind listed the various ways he'd chosen Nick over her. She tried to tell herself she was being illogical, but she'd always come back to the manuscript. To how he hadn't told her Nick had read it, that he'd sent it to their agent.

Keeping that from her had not been protecting her, even if he'd thought it was. It had done more harm than good, and she couldn't be sure that he wouldn't do something similar in the future.

She would have kept sulking on Christmas Eve, except Dylan dragged her out of bed and made her shower. "You're coming over for a slumber party," she said. "Frankie and I got a tree, and we haven't decorated it yet. You're going to help us, and we're going to order Chinese food. Then tomorrow, we're going to open gifts and eat a fantastic dinner that I ordered because I don't want to spend the whole damn day cooking. Plus, there's your cake." Her tone left no room to argue.

Being around Dylan, Frankie, and the dogs improved Evvie's mood, and she enjoyed decorating the tree with them.

Every few minutes, though, she thought about how she had planned to spend the day with Matthias. Not only with him, but with Loretta, Bea, and Sophie too. She pictured them laughing together, watching movies, playing in the snow. Tomorrow, they'd open gifts, and Sophie would open the coloring set Evvie had given to Bea for her. Evvie still had gifts for Matthias, Bea, and Loretta at her house that she would likely never give them now.

Whenever Dylan noticed Evvie faltering, she'd ask a Christmas trivia question to distract her. It worked to a degree, and Evvie was grateful for it.

The next day, Dylan and Frankie woke her up at ten by singing "Happy Birthday." They brought her breakfast in bed, a candle stuck into a stack of pancakes, the whole dish dotted with sprinkles.

Evvie sat up and blew out the candle, smiling at her friends. Even though her eyes were swollen and itchy from crying herself to sleep, she was glad she'd slept at Dylan's and not at her home, alone.

It wasn't the Christmas or the birthday she'd wished for, but she was still happy with what she'd got.

CHAPTER THIRTY

MATTHIAS

On Christmas Eve, Sophie insisted on watching all the *Santa Clause* movies. Matthias tried to pay attention, but all he could think about was Evvie. She was supposed to be there with him and his family, celebrating the day together.

But he'd hidden what Nick had done from her, and then he'd tried to play it off like it was no big deal. He should have been honest with her as soon as he'd found out what had happened. He hadn't thought through what keeping it secret meant, what it would mean to her as someone who valued honesty so highly. As someone whose last partner had kept secrets.

Etta and Bea were preparing homemade pizzas for dinner when there was a knock at the door. Matthias ignored it, so Etta went to answer it.

He was still zoned out when Etta put a hand on his shoulder. "Hey," she said softly. "It's Nick. He wants to talk, and I think you should let him."

Matthias turned to look at her. "*You* think I should talk to Nick?"

She nodded. "It's Christmas Eve, Matthias."

Sighing, he grabbed his cane and pushed himself to his feet.

"We'll talk outside," he said to Nick in greeting as he grabbed his jacket. Nick had bags under his eyes and a five o'clock shadow.

Matthias closed the front door behind him and brushed the snow off one of the porch chairs. Nick did the same to the one beside it, and they both sat.

"Happy Christmas Eve, Matty," Nick said. When Matthias didn't respond, he continued, "I'm sorry. I'm an asshole. I shouldn't have done what I did, and there's no excuse for it. I mean, I did have a reason, but it was a stupid one, clearly." He paused. "I talked to Evvie a few days ago."

Matthias shot him a look, but before he could say anything, Nick continued, "I ran into her in town. I apologized to her, and I told her it was entirely my fault. That you weren't involved at all."

Matthias leaned his head against the chair. "That's great, Nick, but she broke up with me."

"I know, man, and I'm sorry. I didn't . . . I told her she should undo that, but she said, *I can't*." Another pause. "I just want you to be happy."

Matthias blew out a breath. This was Nick to a tee. Messing up royally, trying to fix it, unable to fix it, apologizing, and being so damn earnest that you couldn't help but forgive him. He never meant any harm, and that was the worst part. Matthias wanted to hate him, wanted to stay mad at him, but he never could. They were brothers. And although Nick's mistake had sparked the break-up, Matthias had been the one who'd kept information from Evvie and defended what Nick had done.

"Thanks," he said. As he prepared to make his offer, he crossed his fingers that Nick wasn't going to do something else stupid in the next few days. "Do you want to come back here? Spend the holidays with us?"

Nick swallowed hard, and Matthias hoped he wasn't going to start crying; he'd felt enough emotions in the last few days to last a lifetime, and he was done with that.

"You sure?" Nick asked.

"Yeah, yeah, I'm sure. Knowing you, you probably already have your stuff in the car."

Nick looked sheepishly at the Uber idling in the driveway, and they both laughed. "I was kinda hoping you wouldn't leave me hanging."

∼

CHRISTMAS WENT WELL. Nick was on his best behavior, helping in the kitchen and coloring with Sophie—with her new book and pencil crayon set from Evvie. When she opened it, Matthias's heart ached. He wished Evvie had been there to give it to Sophie herself.

On Christmas Day—Evvie's birthday—Nick hid the pickle in the tree so he wouldn't be eligible for the prize, and he beat the spätzle for Etta until he said his arm was about to fall off. Matthias couldn't tell if he was doing it all to apologize or out of a genuine desire to be helpful, but either way, everyone seemed content to have him around. It meant Matthias didn't have to beat the spätzle, anyway, which gave him time to spend with Sophie. She painted his nails bright pink.

That night, Sophie asked Matthias to read her a bedtime story. "Of course, baby," he said, making himself comfortable beside her in the double bed she shared with Bea. She snuggled against him as they read two stories together—one about a precocious axolotl, and another about a cat who saved a library.

"All sleepy now?" Matthias asked her as he tucked her in.

She made a little humming noise. "Opa, can you rub my back until I fall asleep?"

Bea usually did that for her, and it touched him that Sophie wanted him to do it tonight. "Sure, sure." He flicked the lights off and sat beside her once again, moving his hand in circles on her back, listening to her breathing slow as she drifted off.

His mother had put him and Etta to sleep this way when they

were kids, and he'd done it for his kids too, as often as he could. Which hadn't been nearly enough.

Once he was sure Sophie was asleep, he eased up off the bed and snuck out of the room, closing the door softly behind him. Bea met him in the hall. "She's asleep," he whispered.

"Thank you," she said, and he followed her to the kitchen for a cup of tea. Etta had gone to bed early, and Nick was outside vaping.

As Bea made the tea, she smiled at him. "Thank you for all of this, Dad. Sophie told me this morning that this was the best Chrismakkah ever." She laughed softly.

His eyes watered, and he turned his head so she wouldn't see. "Did you enjoy it too?"

Bea set a steaming mug in front of him. "Of course I did. It's always a treat when I get to spend time with you."

He took her hand, giving it a squeeze. "I'm sorry I wasn't a better father when you were growing up. I'm trying to be better now, for you and for Sophie."

Bea's eyebrows pinched together. "Dad . . . you've always been a good father." He must have looked confused because she continued, "I might not have had the most normal childhood, with all the traveling and having a rock star for a dad, but you were there for me when I needed you. You took me on vacations, I got to see many of your shows, and you came home when you could."

"Was that enough, though? Weren't you ever upset that I wasn't at your talent shows or soccer games?" All those occasions he'd missed and sometimes hadn't even thought of because he'd been so busy.

"Well, yeah, I was sad sometimes. But you were following your dreams. You set that example for me—that nothing was out of reach. No dream was too big for me, ever. Not when I had you to look up to. Did I miss you? Of course. But the important thing is that you tried, you put in effort and showed me you *wanted* to be there even when you couldn't be. And you showed up when you could."

His throat tightened with tears. Hearing his daughter say she looked up to him . . . It meant more than she would ever know.

She patted his shoulder. "I understand better now with Sophie, with her father leaving us." She paused. Matthias knew Sophie's dad was a touchy subject. "But I think I knew it even then. None of us can be perfect parents, or perfect people in any way. What matters is that we keep trying, keep striving to be better even when we know perfection is unachievable."

That's what he'd done, what he'd been doing for years. But he'd still felt that pressure to be perfect, and it had come from himself.

"Thank you, baby," he said, hugging her. They hadn't had many heart-to-hearts on this level, and he wanted to film this moment and replay it over and over.

"If you want more quiet vacations like this, though, I'd be happy with that too." After a moment of comfortable silence, she said, "How are you doing? You've been a bit quiet since . . . you know."

Since his last phone call with Evvie. "I'm sorry. I've been trying to keep my spirits up, but—"

"Dad, you don't need to apologize. I know you miss her. Everything seemed to be going so well between you. Do you want to talk about what happened?"

He shook his head. He hadn't told anyone the details. Bea and Etta knew he'd fought with Nick, but he wasn't sure if they'd pieced together that it had something to do with Evvie. And he didn't want to dredge up what Nick had done again. That was in the past.

"Okay. Well, if you do want to talk, I'm here. Even after we leave tomorrow, you can always call me, okay? We're not that far, now that you're living up here."

"Thanks, baby." Etta hadn't told Matthias he could live there officially, but he'd made himself comfortable, and he wasn't planning to get on the plane with Nick for LA—whenever Nick decided to leave, or Etta kicked the old codger out.

Bea went to bed a few minutes later and Nick came inside, stomping the snow off his boots.

He and Matthias were the last two awake, and Nick conjured a bottle of whiskey from somewhere, offering Matthias a glass. They sat on the couch with the lights off, but the tree lit the whole room.

"What's up?" Nick asked him.

Matthias sipped his drink, knowing Nick was asking about one topic in particular. "I wish I was with her, but what can I do about it? She doesn't want to be with me."

"Hmm." Nick swirled the whiskey around in his glass. "Will you tell me about her?"

The question took Matthias by surprise. He didn't think he wanted to talk about her, but now that Nick had given him the opportunity, he found that he did. He told Nick about how they got together, how Evvie was such a good listener as long as she had something to fidget with. He talked about the market, finding a tree, and going to queer seniors' night with her.

"Man, I'm proud of you," Nick said when Matthias was done. "Past-you wouldn't have gone to a queer seniors' night."

Matthias huffed out a laugh. "There's something you should probably know." He veered away from talking about Evvie to recount how he'd gone to that gay club and Colin had asked him not to do that again.

"Are you serious?" Nick yelled. Matthias shushed him. "Sorry. That's bullshit, man! We need to have a conversation with Colin. I can't believe he did that. I can't believe you didn't tell me!"

"It didn't seem important at the time." In fact, it had seemed important that he *didn't* tell anyone. Coming out to Nick and Steven had been difficult enough.

Nick lightly punched Matthias's arm. "If it was important to you, it's important to me. Fucking Colin." He shook his head. "Anyway, you were talking about Evvie."

Matthias continued to spill everything, and the more he spoke, the more his chest hurt, like his heart was literally breaking, crumbling into pieces over the relationship he'd lost. "I miss her," he said.

"I think you can get her back."

"What? Nick, please don't start scheming again—"

"I'm not. I'm just saying, I think it's possible."

"She told you she didn't want to get back together with me."

"That's not exactly what she said. And I don't think that's true."

"What do you mean?"

As Nick stared at the tree, the lights reflected in his glasses' lenses. "It doesn't seem like she's got anything to be unhappy about when it comes to you."

Matthias focused on the burn in his chest, his favorite part of drinking whiskey, as he poured himself another drink. "Then why won't she take me back?"

"I think this whole thing with the manuscript spooked her. You said she had trust issues because of something that happened with her ex, right?" Nick asked. Matthias nodded. "Well, she trusted you with her manuscript, then I went and showed it to someone she didn't trust. And she definitely doesn't trust me. I think that scared her."

That wasn't the most illogical thing Nick had ever said. Surprisingly, it made sense. "So . . . I need to show her she can trust me?"

"Ehh." Nick tilted his head side to side. "Not necessarily. But I think you need to show her you care about her, that you're willing to put in the work, and you want her to give you a second chance."

"How the hell do you mess up so badly and then give advice like this?" Matthias snorted. "We've known each other for decades, and you still surprise me."

"What can I say? It's a talent." Nick preened.

Rolling his eyes, Matthias said, "So how do I show her how much I care? What can I do to win her back?"

"I dunno, man," Nick said. They were quiet for a few

minutes. Nick stuck his hands in his pockets—a move he often used during silences that stretched too long—then frowned, pulling out a piece of crumpled paper and throwing it on the table.

Matthias caught sight of a logo on the paper. He leaned forward and uncrumpled it, revealing one of the flyers he'd seen in town for Creekfest, Juniper Creek's New Year's Eve celebration in the park.

The festival hadn't existed when he was a kid, but Etta had told him about it. The town set up a stage, invited a few bands from the area to play—usually up-and-coming groups—and set off fireworks at the stroke of midnight. Earlier, Matthias had asked Etta if she wanted to go this year, and she'd said no because it was too loud. "And I'll be in bed by ten," she'd added.

The thought of the festival sparked an idea, and Matthias got a boost of energy. "I think I know how to win Evvie back. You up for helping?"

"Always," Nick said, turning to give him his full attention. "What do you need me to do?"

Matthias was going to show Evvie he cared. He was going to put his heart out there just like she had, and he was going to show her he was enough for her. He wanted to be someone she could trust, so he would put in the work. He would right what was wrong. He would get her back.

CHAPTER THIRTY-ONE

EVVIE

On Boxing Day morning, Evvie and Dylan sat at Dylan's kitchen table with cups of coffee, munching on cinnamon buns Evvie had made the night before. Not wanting to be alone, she'd stayed another night at her friends'. Darcy, one of Dylan's dogs, had draped herself across Evvie's feet. Frankie had a headache and was still in bed, so they kept their voices down.

"Thank you for not letting me waste away in bed," Evvie said, licking icing off her finger.

Dylan waved a hand. "You'd do the same for me. In fact, you *have* done that for me before. Are you doing okay?"

Evvie put another cinnamon bun on her plate. "I didn't cry myself to sleep last night, so that's an improvement."

Dylan narrowed her eyes, her gaze going fuzzy as she stared at a spot over Evvie's shoulder. Evvie let her think, knowing she'd voice her thoughts if they were important. When Dylan refocused, she said, "Are you sure breaking up with Matthias was what you wanted?"

Evvie almost choked, and she coughed a couple times to clear her throat. "What do you mean?" she asked, her eyes watering.

"I don't want to overstep," Dylan said. "This might be something you should talk about with your therapist. But . . . he made you happy. Happier than I've seen you in a while, and that's saying something."

Heat rose in Evvie's chest. Dylan meant well, but she wasn't in Evvie's head or body. She couldn't feel what Evvie felt—the crushing in her ribs when she'd opened the email from the agent, the nausea when she'd realized it had had something to do with Matthias. Yes, Nick had been the one to send the manuscript, but Matthias had known about it, and he hadn't told her. He hadn't even planned to tell her, and the only reason she found out was the email. At least if she'd known what Nick had done, she could have prepared herself for the agent's response.

"I was happy with him." She avoided Dylan's gaze. "I thought maybe . . . Well, it doesn't matter now. But breaking up with him was the right thing to do. It's better for me this way."

The look Dylan gave her was somewhere between *I don't believe you* and *You're lying to yourself*, but Evvie ignored it.

"I don't need someone else to be happy," she said firmly. "I've been fine on my own for decades, and I'll be peachy again in no time." Even if sleeping with another person had been a nice change.

Dylan stacked their empty plates. "You're right, you don't need someone else to be happy. But don't deny yourself something because you're scared of it. Look at me and Frankie. I could have told her to shove it when she came back, but I didn't. The risk was there, and still is there, that she'd leave again. But I won't deny myself happiness *just in case*. You can't live like that, Evvie."

Was that what she was doing? Denying herself happiness with Matthias because she didn't want her trust broken again? But it *had* been broken. It wasn't a "just in case." It was a proven fact, as real as the dog lying across her feet.

"Dylan," Frankie called from upstairs. "Can you please bring me a painkiller?"

"Yeah, just a sec," Dylan called back.

Evvie scooched her chair out and stood, apologizing to Darcy as she did so. "I should get going," she said. "And let you take care of your partner. I want to try working on my novel again, anyway."

"Ready to write the last chapters?" Dylan asked as she stuck their plates in the sink.

If Evvie was going to meet her goal of finishing the book before the new year, she only had a few days left. "Yes." She set her jaw. "I am."

THE WORDS WEREN'T COMING, and Evvie had been staring at her laptop screen for way too long. Every time she tried to focus on the story, her mind drifted somewhere else.

She pulled out her notebook, going over the notes she'd taken from her not-real-dates and then a couple real dates with Matthias. About what they'd done and how she'd felt. They hadn't gone to the paint night or done the light walk like she'd wanted, but she still had plenty to work with. Those notes helped her understand her characters, yet she was still stuck on the reconciliation scene.

The irony wasn't lost on her that she'd just experienced her own break-up and was stuck in the same spot as her protagonist. Her heroine had decided not to pursue a relationship with the pie maker because his ex-fiancée had come to town wanting to get back together with him—an ex-fiancée that he'd never mentioned.

Evvie sighed as she stared at the screen. Maybe she needed a fresh perspective.

She opened her email and found the first one where Dylan gave her in-depth feedback. These emails had been taunting her, but she'd feared what they would say, even if she trusted her best friend wholeheartedly. With a deep breath, she opened the first email and read it.

Most of Dylan's comments were positive, and her suggestions weren't that bad at all. With her anxiety cooling, Evvie opened the next email, then the next. Nothing hurt the way she thought it would . . . until she got to the last email. The one where Dylan commented on the break-up scene.

So, she breaks up with him out of self-preservation, right? Dylan wrote. *That's understandable, but she needs to move past that. He kept that secret because he didn't want to hurt her, which ultimately shows how much he cares. It might not have been the right thing to do, but somehow she needs to realize that she can't sabotage herself based on possibilities.*

Evvie put her face in her hands and groaned.

Her heart pounding, she skimmed through the break-up scene and the following ones where her heroine thought everything was over. It was like reading a reflection of herself, a mirror image of her own life. Her fears, right there on the page.

They were exactly what Dylan had said they were.

If Evvie had read the feedback earlier, would she have reacted to the manuscript incident the same way? Would she have broken up with Matthias at all?

All these thoughts and feelings were overwhelming, and she needed a break. She pulled out the flour and sugar, her mind still on her story.

As she was rolling out cookie dough, a light bulb went on in her brain. The heroine thought she wanted to win the baking show when what she really wanted was to be with the pie maker. And to be with him, to truly trust him, she needed to move on from her ex-husband and set the insecurities he'd given her aside. The approval she'd been seeking wasn't from other people, but from herself.

Evvie knew exactly how the story needed to end.

Leaving the cookie dough on the counter, she rushed over to her laptop and cracked her knuckles then started typing, her fingers flying across the keyboard. She wasn't thinking so much as relaying the information at this point, letting the story do what it needed to do.

When she finished, she took a deep breath and looked at the

clock. Two hours had passed, but her manuscript was complete! She whooped and did a little dance in the kitchen.

She knew her protagonist better than ever before, had felt exactly what she'd felt, had connected with her so deeply. Evvie's insecurities had been her own roadblock with this story, and as soon as she backed out of her own way, the path had been clear and easy to follow.

The missing link had been her belief in herself. Her confidence. Listening to her best friend had shown her that.

And now she knew how to move forward in her own life as well.

CHAPTER THIRTY-TWO

MATTHIAS

New Year's Eve had often been a more momentous December occasion than Christmas or Hanukkah for Matthias since everyone in LA loved to party. They had no shortage of events to choose from every year, and Nick sometimes threw one of his own.

Creekfest was a party, but it wasn't as big or as flashy as the ones in LA. Banners were strung along the stage displaying logos of the local sponsors: Get Your Gear, Cedar Logs art gallery, The June Bug diner, The Tabby Cat café, and Yellow Brick Books.

Despite Etta's earlier insistence that she wouldn't go to Creekfest, she stood with Matthias and Nick backstage, earplugs in, gripping Matthias's arm. He'd told her she didn't have to come, but she'd insisted on being there. She'd even dressed up more than usual and put on makeup.

"Thank you for letting us do this last minute," Matthias said to Lorelai, the mayor of Juniper Creek, who was explaining to them how everything would work. She wore a gray Creekfest shirt, and she'd proudly told them how a local high school student, Kat, had designed the logo for the festival.

"Of course," she said. "I couldn't say no to a pitch like yours.

We've slotted you in between the second and third acts, so be prepared for your signal."

It would be strange to perform without Steven, but it wasn't like they were doing a full set. Matthias wouldn't even be playing drums, and he hadn't realized until then that his drums had been somewhat of a safety net for him. Tonight it would be Nick with his guitar and microphone, and Matthias with a microphone. That was it.

After Bea and Sophie left, the two of them had worked their asses off to get this right. Nick had been so focused, Matthias was reminded of the early Iridium Twilight days when they had been trying to get their first record deal. The pressure had been high, and the stakes had felt like the end of the world.

While his livelihood wasn't on the line, this performance felt even more important. His heart was at risk now.

"You ready?" Nick asked, bouncing on the balls of his feet. "This crowd may be small, but there's energy out there, man. You feel it?" Nick may have been in his late sixties, but at times like this, Matthias was sure he reverted to his twenties.

All Matthias felt were the butterflies in his stomach. What if he opened his mouth and instead of words coming out, he unleashed something far less savory? He asked Etta if she could find him a bottle of water and she took off, probably glad for something to do.

Waiting in the wings was agony, and he tried not to poke his head on stage to look at the crowd. He was counting on Dylan to get Evvie there. If she didn't show up, all of this was for nothing. Dylan had seemed over the moon that he'd asked her for a favor, though, and he assured himself it would all work out.

He barely heard the first act play, and when the second act started, he followed their songs on the program as if his life depended on it. Etta returned with water for him, and he chugged the whole thing.

"We're up next, Matty," Nick said, elbowing him in the ribs.

"I know," Matthias replied breathlessly.

Lorelai stepped on stage after the second act, thanking them and reading out a spiel from one of the sponsors; she reminded the crowd that The June Bug was open late if people needed a warm drink or a pastry.

Matthias willed his lungs to take in more air, and before he knew it, he was following Nick on stage.

The crowd was small, but still a crowd, still large enough that he couldn't find Evvie as his eyes shifted from person to person. It didn't help that the stage lights were bright against the dark sky, making him wish for sunglasses.

This is just like any other show, he told himself. Although it wasn't, not in the slightest.

"Hello, Juniper Creek!" Nick said into his microphone, eliciting cheers and whistles from the crowd. "You might know us from a little band called Iridium Twilight." More cheers, this time even louder.

Matthias still couldn't find Evvie.

"Tonight, we're not here as a rock band, but as a couple of average guys on a mission." He gestured for Matthias to take over.

Matthias cleared his throat, desperately searching the crowd. He couldn't stall any longer, not without making things awkward. This was it. Now or never.

"Evvie Adler, if you're out there, I want you to know how sorry I am. I want to be honest with you forever and always. This one's for you."

CHAPTER THIRTY-THREE

EVVIE

*E*vvie hadn't missed a Creekfest in decades, but she wasn't sure if she wanted to go anywhere this year. She'd even skipped the most recent queer seniors' meeting because she hadn't felt ready to talk to her friends, to answer their questions about Matthias, to come up with a high and a low for the holidays.

She'd been doing some soul searching since her epiphany, journaling and talking to her therapist. Her instinct had been to rush to Matthias, to apologize and ask if they could be partners again, but she felt like she needed time.

Time to absorb what she had learned. Time to come to terms with herself, and to figure out what she truly wanted. She didn't want to jump headfirst into a relationship again and then second-guess her choices.

If she was going to be with Matthias, she wanted to be *sure* of it. There could be no doubt in her mind.

On New Year's Eve, Dylan and Frankie stood on her front step, staring at her. Dylan's brows shot up. "What do you mean you aren't coming?" They usually left early for the celebration so they could stand up front near the stage. It was difficult to push through the crowd once your feet hurt, but it was worth the view until they got too tired.

"I was thinking of having a bubble bath instead," Evvie said. "Having a reflective, contemplative New Year's Eve for a change."

Dylan's jaw dropped. "You're fucking kidding me."

"Hey," Frankie said, putting her hand on Dylan's arm. "If she wants to stay home, let her stay home."

"No. Nope. Not happening. Evvie, you have to be there."

"You don't even like Creekfest." Evvie waved them off. Dylan had tried to get out of going multiple years previously, and Evvie had dragged her along. Why was everything backward this year?

"Exactly," Dylan said. "I don't. Which is why you have to be there. Come on, this is Frankie's first big Juniper Creek event. Don't you want to show her all the cool stuff that I'll overlook? Plus, Kat designed the logo this year. Don't you want to support them?"

Technically, Pumpkin Days in October had been Frankie's first big Juniper Creek event, but Dylan had a good point. She was terrible at noticing the little things, always pushing ahead to the main attraction and forgetting to enjoy the rest of it. And of course Evvie wanted to support Kat.

"Ugh, fine. Give me a few minutes to get dressed."

They drove over in Dylan's truck, arriving later than usual. They couldn't get to the front of the crowd, and they ended up right in the middle where you felt the most invisible but also the most present. Evvie didn't love it—all the pointy elbows and taller people blocking her view—but she'd deal with it until at least the second act. Then maybe she could sneak out.

The first group was an indie folk band with Celtic influences, their music light and easy to listen to. As Evvie watched them play, she focused on the drummer, thinking of Matthias.

She wondered what he was doing this evening. What if he was at Creekfest? That hadn't occurred to her before, and she was suddenly aware of everyone around her. What would she do if she ran into him? She wasn't prepared for that.

As the first band finished their set and the crowd cheered,

Evvie leaned over to Dylan and said, "I'm getting tired already. I might move to the back of the crowd."

Dylan's eyes grew wide, and she grabbed Evvie's arm. "You need to stay here. Please."

"Are you alright?"

Dylan seemed panicky, which was odd for her. Frankie had clearly noticed as well since she was frowning at Dylan.

"I'm fine," Dylan said. "Let's go to the back, then. But can we stay at least until the end of the second act? I . . . I've heard them before."

"I suppose." Why was Dylan acting so strange? Evvie shot Frankie a look, but Frankie shrugged.

They pushed through the crowd to the back, close to where the drink tents were set up. Eleanor's daughter, Vera, was serving alcohol there along with a few other employees from Juniper Foods. Another tent nearby had a Tabletop Time banner across the front; Hijiri and Iris, the owners of the board game store, were selling glowsticks and other flashy concert gadgets.

The second act started—a country group with songs about trucks and summer love. Dylan didn't listen to country. Evvie narrowed her eyes at her friend, but Dylan was focused on the stage. Almost *too* focused. Like she was pretending.

Evvie shook her head but went with it. She didn't mind country music.

"I think they're selling T-shirts and CDs at the side there," Frankie said once the set was done. "Want me to get us a CD?" she asked Dylan.

"Oh, god no," Dylan replied, making a disgusted face. Evvie and Frankie looked at each other again, and Dylan said, "I mean, sure. Yes. They were great. But I think I'd prefer one of the Creekfest T-shirts."

Evvie crossed her arms. "You've always been an incompetent liar. What's going on?"

"Oh, for fuck's sake." Dylan rolled her eyes. "I'm the worst fucking person for this. Trust me, okay? We need to stand here for a few more minutes."

"And you don't want that CD," Frankie said.

"I really don't," Dylan replied.

Evvie was exasperated, but Dylan had asked them to trust her, so she would. Even if all she wanted to do was go home and have a bath. She'd even bought herself a cotton candy bath bomb with sprinkles in it for the occasion.

She was telling Frankie about one of last year's groups when the crowd cheered again. Two people had just walked on stage.

One stepped up to the main microphone and said, "Hello, Juniper Creek!" Why did that voice sound familiar? "You might know us from a little band called Iridium Twilight."

Dylan nudged Evvie, and Evvie turned to the stage. Her gaze zeroed in on the person, but they were standing too far back in the crowd for her to see details. She was sure that was Nick, though. Which meant the other person was probably . . .

"Tonight, we're not here as a rock band, but as a couple of average guys on a mission."

The other person on stage had been hanging back, but now they stepped forward, leaning on a cane, and said, "Evvie Adler, if you're out there, I want you to know how sorry I am. I want to be honest with you forever and always. This one's for you."

At the sound of Matthias's voice, Evvie's heart just about stopped. Had he just apologized to her in front of the whole town then dedicated a song to her?

Without consciously deciding to do so, she pushed through the crowd, using her elbows to squish through even though she hated when other people did that. Right now, she didn't care. She needed to get to the front.

The sound of Nick's guitar filled the air as he played a sweet, slow melody. Matthias was the first to sing, his voice gravelly in a pleasant way that Evvie felt in her bones. She had no idea he could sing like that, and it threatened to turn her to jelly. The song was clearly about a relationship, about trusting someone with the vulnerable pieces of you.

Evvie continued wading through people until she reached the front. Matthias and Nick were partway through the chorus, harmonizing. The way their voices wove together brought her to tears.

Nick sang the second verse as Matthias tapped out the beat with his foot, taking the audience on a journey through the relationship. When the two men sang together once again for the chorus, Evvie let the words flow over her:

> I've hurt and been hurt, but with you I'm free,
> With you by my side, I'm where I'm meant to be.
> I'm trusting you with my heart, and I know it's
>   worth it,
> Cause with you, I've found love, and I'll never
>   regret it.

Her tears overflowed, spilling down her cheeks. She smiled at the stage, and Matthias looked directly at her. The exact moment she caught his eye, his expression turned earnest, and he walked forward until he was clearly singing directly to her. The bridge of the song had clever word play related to writing that made her laugh, and then that last chorus . . .

He sang, "Cause with you, I've found love, and I'll never regret it."

Evvie practically sobbed with happiness, and one of the security guards at the front moved the metal barricade so she could get by. She ran around to the side of the stage and up the stairs, straight into Matthias's arms.

The crowd went wild.

CHAPTER THIRTY-FOUR

MATTHIAS

*H*e hadn't seen her until the second verse. Then there she was, front and center, beaming up at him. She was wearing her pink coat, which stood out in the crowd, so she must not have been there earlier.

He sang the rest of the song directly to her, Nick's voice coming in to complement his for the last chorus. As he sang the last line to Evvie, he put his heart and soul into it. "Cause with you, I've found love, and I'll never regret it." They may not have known each other for long, but he felt those words with every fiber of his being. He loved her.

And he hoped she felt the same.

When the song finished, the last notes of the guitar fading away, Evvie ran around to the side of the stage and bolted up the stairs. He wasn't sure what to expect, but she flung herself into his arms, almost knocking him over. Nick took the microphone from him, laughing and clapping along with the crowd.

"I'm so sorry," Matthias said into Evvie's hair. She smelled like cookie dough and the cherry blossom soap she used. "Please forgive me."

She leaned back and took his face between her palms, her blue eyes sparkling. "Of course I do. I'm sorry too." She brought her face to meet his, their lips colliding as the crowd hooted.

Evvie giggled against his mouth then pulled back. "We should probably take this off stage."

"Probably," he said, kissing her again for good measure.

The two of them walked off hand in hand, Nick right behind them. Etta waited for them on the lawn behind the stage, grinning. Evvie let go of Matthias to hug his sister.

"So that means it worked?" Etta asked.

"It worked." Evvie turned around and pulled Nick into a hug as well. "That was sweeter than Aaliyah's best pie," she said, wiping her eyes. "Thank you, both."

"Matty helped with the lyrics, which he *never* does," Nick replied. "You've brought that old man out of his shell."

"Who are you calling *old*?" Matthias scowled. He shifted his body weight to push Nick over slightly, and his friend laughed.

Evvie reached for Matthias's hand again and held it tightly as if she never wanted to let go, which was a-okay with him. "Are your fingernails pink?" she asked, laughing.

"Yep," he said proudly. "Sophie painted them. Do you like it?"

"I love it." She raised his hand to her mouth and kissed the back of it. "Want to watch the fireworks? I know the perfect spot."

"Yeah, yeah." He'd follow her anywhere. "Nick? Etta? You coming?"

As a group, they followed Evvie toward the library.

"You got Dylan involved with this, didn't you?" Evvie asked him as they walked. He kept her as close to him as he could, enjoying having her near again.

"Maybe. Why?"

"She was acting so strange earlier, but now it makes sense."

He smiled coyly. "I might have gone to the library yesterday and recruited her help. Just in case you wouldn't be here."

She rested her head on his arm. "I almost didn't show, you know. So it's a good thing you had a plan."

Thank god he did. He had no idea what he would have done if the song had finished and she hadn't been there.

They walked past the library to the playground beyond, where Dylan and another woman sat on the swings. Evvie introduced the woman as Frankie, Dylan's girlfriend.

"Look at you and all your queer friends," Nick said, nudging Matthias.

Matthias didn't bother explaining that this was the first time he'd met Frankie. Supportive Nick was a good Nick.

"Why are we at the park, exactly?" Etta asked, sitting on the empty swing beside Frankie. She pushed off with her feet, her hair flowing in the breeze.

"Library secret," Dylan said. "We get the best view of the fireworks from here." She stood, sticking her hands in her pockets as she came over to Nick and Matthias. "Sorry if this is weird, but I am a huge fan. Could I maybe get an autograph later?"

"Of course!" Nick said, always ready to please his fans.

Matthias nodded. "Sure, sure."

Evvie squeezed his hand and mouthed *Thank you* at him as Dylan went back to the swing.

Nick climbed the play structure and sat at the top of the slide with his legs stretched out, while Evvie and Matthias sat on one of the low platforms.

Matthias put his arm around Evvie, pulling her close and kissing the top of her head. "This isn't a dream, is it?" he asked. She pinched his arm. "Ow!"

"Nope," she said, the dimple on her cheek as prominent as ever. "It's not a dream. And I'm not going anywhere."

"I sure hope not." He leaned down to kiss her. "I'm not going anywhere either."

"Get a room!" Nick called, making the entire group laugh.

The fireworks started; red, blue, green, and white shapes exploded against the stars and cascaded from the sky in shimmers.

Even with his aching leg and his cold nose, Matthias never

wanted to move from that spot. He held Evvie tight, watched the sky light up, listened to Nick rating the fireworks, and brought in the new year with a kiss.

EPILOGUE

EVVIE

"*E*vvie?" Matthias called from Evvie's kitchen downstairs. "You ready to go? We're going to be late."

"Almost!" Evvie gathered her hair and clipped it against the back of her head, letting pieces fall down the front. The holidays were over but it was still winter, so she put her glittery snowflake earrings on while she walked down the stairs. "Got the cookies?"

"Right here," he said, shaking the container and making the cookies rattle. He was in his coat and boots already, gloves on, standing in front of the door.

"How do I look?" she asked, holding out her arms and swaying. Her sweater was white with glimmering silver threads woven throughout it, and her leggings were bright blue.

"Beautiful, as always," Matthias replied. "Although, I would prefer less."

She froze. "Less?"

"Less clothes. No sweater, no leggings, you can maybe keep the socks, though . . ."

"Matthias!" She scowled playfully at him. "Save that kind of talk for after the meeting."

In the car, Evvie put on an early Iridium Twilight album.

Matthias raised his eyebrows at her. "Apparently this is Dylan's favorite album."

"Ah. I'll have to get her a signed copy of this one, then, in addition to the one Nick gave her. I can give it to her with the completed band memoir."

"All the material is in?" Evvie asked. Matthias had sent his completed story to their agent before the New Year's Eve celebration, but Nick was late with his.

Matthias nodded. "It's all with the ghostwriter! They should really be called a *rearranger*—it's not like they're writing any of it."

"That's still a difficult job, I'm sure," Evvie said.

"Oh, of course. And I'm sure you could give them a few pointers."

She glanced at him fondly. He'd read the rest of her manuscript earlier in the week, and he'd loved it. She didn't want to rely totally on his feedback, though. He was her partner, after all, so he was biased.

They were the last people to arrive at the meeting. "Matthias! Good to see you again," Priya called from the circle of chairs.

"And you brought cookies," Gem said, getting up to greet them.

They took a few minutes to get settled. Tom didn't remember Matthias, so they reintroduced him. Then they went through their highs and lows, Evvie insisting she go last.

Matthias went right before her. "My low was saying goodbye to my daughter and granddaughter last week. They spent the holidays with us, but my daughter is a nurse and had to get back to work. And my high was the Creekfest celebration. I loved one of the bands, and the fireworks after were incredible." He winked at Evvie.

Gem pressed her lips together; she had been at the celebration with Margie, so she knew Matthias was part of Iridium Twilight. She had promised to keep it quiet until he was ready to share, even though the local paper had already published an article about it. "Evvie?" she asked.

"My low was forgetting a bunch of cookie dough on the counter and having to throw it out. But I have lots of highs to make up for it. Creekfest and the fireworks are two of them. But also, I finished my manuscript!"

Gem clapped, Priya whooped, and Noah said, "Good for you!" Tom nodded along, hopefully remembering she was writing a story but possibly not.

"Matthias and Dylan have read it, but I'd like to get more feedback before I decide what to do with it. Gem and Priya, I know you like romance books. Would you be willing to give it a readthrough for me?"

"I've enjoyed a romance novel or two in my time," Noah said. "Can I also read it?"

"Of course!" Evvie said. "Tom?"

Tom wrinkled his nose. "I prefer thrillers."

She handed out three copies of her manuscript, making her tote bag that much lighter. "If you don't like it, that's alright; you are not obligated to finish it. I appreciate any and all feedback."

And she trusted them. All of them. While Nick had upset her, the literary agent's response had shown her there were possibilities for her book. Dylan encouraged her to look into self-publishing as well. There were so many options these days, and she wanted to do her research properly.

"I'm proud of you," Matthias said, leaning over so only she could hear.

"I'm proud of me, too." She pecked him on the cheek.

Priya sighed longingly. "You two are so sweet. I want a romance like yours."

Evvie looked at Matthias right as he looked at her, and they laughed. Evvie didn't cover her mouth, letting her smile shine bright. "It's everything I wished for," she said.

As it turned out, happily-ever-afters *were* meant for her.

WANT MORE JUNIPER CREEK?

Sign up for Brenna Bailey's newsletter so you'll never miss a new release! You'll also get a free, exclusive short story about how Gem and Margie met with your newsletter subscription.

Get your free short story now!
www.brennabailey.com/newsletter

AUTHOR'S NOTE

Thank you for joining me for the winter holidays in Juniper Creek! I hope you felt the holiday spirit and loved Evvie and Matthias as much as I do.

This book means a lot to me. I'm a queer woman married to a queer man, so our queerness is not visible. I've often felt not queer enough because of that, and I worked through many of my own insecurities as I wrote this story. I want to echo the dedication here in case it didn't sink in: To everyone who feels like they aren't enough. I see you, and you *are* enough.

No matter what you thought of *Wishing on Winter*, please help your fellow readers by leaving a review on social media and your favorite reading platforms and stores. Reviews are hugely important for getting books in the hands of the right readers. Cheers!

ACKNOWLEDGMENTS

I am a settler on Turtle Island, and I wrote this book in Moh'kinsstis in the Treaty 7 region of Southern Alberta. This is the traditional territory of the Blackfoot Confederacy, the Tsuut'ina, the Stoney Nakoda Nations, and the Métis Nation of Region 3. The more I learn about this land, the more I appreciate and respect it.

It truly takes a community to write a book, and I have many people to thank for this story.

A huge thank you to everyone who supports me in my daily life. Mom, Dad, Keegan, and Tanya, thank you for keeping me fueled in more ways than one at our weekly dinners. Phoebe and Steph, thank you for reading the worst versions of my stories and still loving me.

Orin, you are the love of my life and the backbone of my creativity. Thank you for taking the time to discuss stories with me! I especially appreciate how you read this book and improved the ADHD representation.

Molly Rookwood, you are a gem of a human! You've been one of my key beta readers from the start, and I always look forward to your feedback. Thank you for bringing your experience as a Jewish sensitivity reader to this story, for helping me develop Matthias and Loretta as Jewish characters.

An enormous thank you to Jacquelynn Lyon and Todd Aasen as well for your invaluable feedback! Jacquelynn, you go above and beyond with your reports, and I am a better writer because of you. Todd, you've been on this journey with me since before I wrote professionally, and discussing stories with you will forever be one of my favorite activities.

Trisha Jenn Loehr, I am honored to call you my book coach and dear friend. I'd be a mess of a romance writer without your encouragement and feedback!

On the topic of messes, Jessica Renwick, I am over the moon that you edited this story for me! Loretta wouldn't have her chickens without you, and the story would have way more repeating words. You've got an eye for detail, and I'm blessed to have you as a friend, colleague, and collaborator.

Talena Winters and Jennifer E. Lindsay, you are both also dear friends, colleagues, and collaborators who have helped me become the author I am today. Our monthly chats (with Jessica, of course!) always boost my writer spirit. And Talena, I am eternally grateful for your book blurb expertise.

Lucy from Cover Ever After, you knew exactly what to do with this cover, and I could not be happier!

A special shout-out to Rosemary Taylor, a member of Rainbow Elders Calgary, for connecting with me and reading this book. I value your feedback and your friendship, and you inspire me with your adventures!

And to my fantastic readers—your reactions to my books make my career worth it. I appreciate your support more than you know!

ALSO BY BRENNA BAILEY

Juniper Creek Golden Years Series

"I Want to Hold Your Hand" (short story)

A Tale of Two Florists

Of Love and Libraries

ABOUT THE AUTHOR

Image Description: Photo of Brenna smiling at the camera. She is a white woman with curly blond hair and glasses, and she's wearing a blue shirt. End of description.

Brenna Bailey writes queer contemporary romance. When she's not writing, she runs an editing business called Bookmarten Editorial. If her nose isn't buried in a book, you can probably find her out in the woods somewhere admiring plants or attempting to identify birds. She is a starry-eyed traveler and a home baker, and she lives in Calgary, Alberta, with her game-loving spouse and their cuddly fur-baby.

instagram.com/brennabaileybooks

Printed in the USA
CPSIA information can be obtained
at www.ICGtesting.com
JSHW011340230324
59619JS00011B/442

9 781778 186783